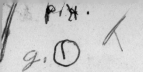

TILL THESE HILLS BE HOME

After her mother's death, Janice Taylor takes a job as housekeeper to Hugh Murray in a Perthshire ski resort, and helps to mother his three children, who's real mother died a year ago.

Janice loves her job and the children, but she must endure many misunderstandings with her male admirers before she eventually finds her true love in the wild beauty of the Scottish hills.

Till These Hills Be Home

by
Janet McKenzie

MAGNA PRINT BOOKS
Long Preston, North Yorkshire,
England.

British Library Cataloguing in Publication Data

McKenzie, Janet
  Till these hills be home.—Large print ed
  I. Title
823′.914(F)   PR6063.C/

  ISBN 0-86009-562-2

First Published in Great Britain 1974

Published in Large Print 1983 by arrangement with The Copyright Holder

Photoset in Great Britain by
Dermar Phototypesetting Co., Long Preston, North Yorkshire.

Printed and bound in Great Britain by
Redwood Burn Limited, Trowbridge.

CHAPTER 1

Janice Taylor drew over into a lay-by, and as she stepped out of the car she took in deep breaths of the fresh hill air. Ever since leaving Perth, she had been conscious of mounting tension, and the doubts about the purpose of her journey.

Be sensible, she told herself now. No-one need know that I'm not just on holiday. If I don't like the hotel, I needn't mention I was ever interested in the job. There won't be any harm done and I can always go back to London.

She took the advertisement which had started it all from her pocket, and read under the 'Situations Vacant' heading:

Competent, kindly woman required to help in management of hotel and care of three young children. Permanent position. Ability to drive and some experience in catering trade preferred. Liking for children essential. Apply to

Hugh Murray, Kirkton House Hotel, Kirkton, by Blairochry, Perthshire.

To Janice, weary after the long months of nursing her mother in their Glasgow flat, and quite alone now after her mother's recent death, the advertisement had been like the answer to a prayer.

She loved the countryside, she had two years' experience of running a restaurant, and she liked children—well, most of them!

Her mother had died eight weeks before, and as there was nothing to keep Janice in Glasgow, she'd decided to look at the hotel in the guise of a casual tourist rather than apply for the job in the conventional way.

As Janice climbed back into the car, she glanced at her watch noting that she'd arrive at the hotel just in time for lunch.

As Janice drove through Blairochry, she slowed down and glanced around the little town, which was the nearest shopping centre to Kirkton House Hotel. It was a pleasant, grey-stone town which had a busy, prosperous air.

8

The hills became higher, and the fields were replaced by moorland as Janice drove farther from the village. When she reached the large hotel sign she turned off the main road on to a twisting, narrow road, and drew up to the large gravelled area in front of Kirkton House Hotel.

As she entered the hotel she was struck by its atmosphere. It was like entering a large, well-kept country house.

'Can I help you?' enquired a pleasant but impersonal male voice. Janice turned to confront a tall, dark-haired man, who, she guessed was Hugh Murray, the advertiser, and, by his proprietary air, the owner of the hotel.

'Yes,' she answered. 'I'd like lunch please—after I've freshened up.'

Almost an hour later, Janice laid down her empty coffee cup and sighed contentedly.

I like it here, she thought. I'll stay the night and, if my first impressions are right, I'll ask about the job tomorrow.

When the waitress came to take her empty cup, Janice enquired if a room was available.

'I'm sure that'll be all right,' said the girl. 'We're very quiet at the moment. If you'll wait a minute, I'll check.' She returned soon and escorted Janice to a brightly furnished bedroom on the first floor.

'Was that the owner of the hotel I spoke to earlier? A tall, dark-haired man?' enquired Janice.

'Ay, that would be Mr Murray right enough.'

'Does Mrs Murray help run the hotel?' asked Janice.

'Oh, dear no,' came the reply. 'Mrs Murray was killed in a car crash last year, and left three lovely bairns without a mother.'

'How tragic!' Janice's voice was low.

'Ay, the whole Glen was awful shocked. The Murrays are well liked here.' The girl drew herself up and added in a business-like tone. 'Dinner is from six o'clock. Will that be all?'

'Yes, thank you.' Janice smiled, silently approving of the girl's reluctance to be drawn into gossip about her employer.

Later, Janice walked up the hill,

behind the hotel and admired the view over Kirkton.

It was on her return that she saw Hugh Murray returning from collecting his family from the village school, and decided that this would be an ideal chance to see the children who might soon be in her charge.

First out of the Land-Rover was a boy of around eight, who jumped down and ran to the side of the hotel. He was followed by a serious-looking little girl, who stepped down carefully and turned round, saying anxiously:

'Careful, now, Robbie!'

This remark was addressed to the third child, a sturdy little boy, who could only just have started school, Janice thought.

When the children had all scampered in by the hotel's side door, Janice moved towards the front. Suddenly aware that she'd been spying, she hurried up to her room to freshen up.

After putting on some fresh lipstick, Janice wondered how to spend the rest of the afternoon. Eventually she decided to drive up the Glen to the steeper slopes, which in a few months would be densely populated by skiers.

At frequent intervals on the road, Janice saw signs of the ski-boom which had recently hit this part of Scotland.

Just a mile above Kirkton House Hotel, a large stone and timber development seemed to be near completion. Many of the cottages too, by the roadside also had newly-built extensions and the traditional Bed and Breakfast signs, often with the words, 'Skiers Welcome,' written below.

Soon Janice reached the bottom station of the ski-lift, which also offered a panoramic view at this time of year. At the top of the lift Janice entered the attractive cedar-wood ski-lift restaurant and ordered a coffee.

As she gazed on the rather bleak outlook, she imagined what it would be like in winter, until a man's voice broke into her thoughts and she turned her head to see the new arrival.

He was leaning on his elbow at the counter, chatting to the girls behind it in a friendly way. His shoulders were broad under the tweed jacket and his trousers were tucked into large wellington boots.

As he turned to glance at her, Janice saw that he had a rugged, outdoor look and a frank, open expression. Something about him appealed to Janice, and she found herself returning his smile.

The feeling she suddenly was aware of, was one she had almost forgotten during the past year.

Before the news of her mother's illness, which had brought her back to Glasgow nine months before, Janice had spent the two previous years running a restaurant in one of London's smartest department stores.

During the second of these years, a new department manager had come to the store and a friendship had slowly developed between Janice and him. Both had enjoyed escaping from London on a Sunday afternoon to walk in fresher air. Bryan was ambitious, and proud that at twenty-five he was manager of the 'Young Man's Boutique', an innovation which was going from strength to strength under his leadership.

Towards the end of her stay in London, Janice had begun to realise that what they felt for each other was more than friendship. Nothing, however, had been put into words. Then suddenly the news had come from Glasgow, and Janice had hurried home, to spend nine months when normal life was suspended.

There had been warm, friendly letters from Bryan, to which Janice had, at the start, replied with equal warmth. As weeks had turned to months, however, everything outside the confines of the Glasgow flat had taken on an air of unreality. Janice would let several weeks pass after hearing from Bryan, before struggling to write a barely adequate reply to his usual warm friendly letter.

Finally, after two of his letters had gone unanswered, Bryan had stopped writing.

When the numbness of her mother's death had begun to wear off a little, Janice had thought of Bryan and had even contemplated returning South.

Tentatively, she had written to Bryan, mentioning her plans. But there had been no reply and pride prevented her writing again. She couldn't blame him for his attitude, but she had expected him to show more understanding. That chapter of her life, she had decided, was closed.

Now, in the restaurant by the chair-lift, the friendly smile from an attractive man warmed her. After bidding the waitress a pleasant goodbye, Janice smiled to herself and felt pleased at the admiring look in the stranger's eyes.

You're twenty-four, she reminded herself as she climbed into the car. Not some teenager having her head turned by a good-looking man who glances twice at her!

Janice had gone only a few miles when she realised that there was something wrong with the car. It gave a few hic-coughs before the engine cut out com-pletely, and came to rest in the middle of one of the few straight stretches on the twisty road.

Janice was a capable motorist who could change a wheel and do most of the maintenance herself, but now she was at a loss to know what was wrong. She sat for a few moments, and after pressing the starter several times, she noticed that the needle on the petrol gauge was as far into the red as it could go. She calculated that the nearest petrol pump was about five miles away, in Kirkton.

Sighing, she went to the boot to fetch an empty petrol can. Leaving the car lights on, as dusk was drawing in, she set off on foot.

Though she didn't intend hitching, she walked on the left-hand-side of the road, in the hope that someone might stop. Two cars passed without slowing, before she heard a vehicle drawing up behind her and a voice hailing her.

'Run out of petrol, have you?'

Turning, Janice recognised the driver as the man from the restaurant.

'I'm afraid so,' she confessed.

'Jump in,' He leant over and opened the door for her. 'We don't need to go to a garage. I always have an extra can of petrol in the back. It's safer, in my line, I never know when I'll be called out.

'Oh, sorry, I should have introduced myself. I'm Sandy Nicol, the local vet.' He gave her a quick smile as he manoeuvred the car up the road.

'I'm Janice Taylor,' she returned. 'I'm staying at Kirkton House Hotel tonight.'

'Oh. Just passing through? Pity. Where are you from?'

'Well, Glasgow, really. But—' Janice broke off, and hesitated, not wanting to confide her plans to this stranger before she even knew if the job was still available.

'I'm really rootless at the moment,' she added lamely, and without explanation.

With this, they reached her car. Soon the gallon of petrol was poured into Janice's tank and when she tried to pay for the petrol, Sandy just smiled.

'Always pleased to help a damsel in distress.' Then he added in a quieter tone, 'I'm sorry your stay is to be so short. Look, here's my card. If you're ever in the district again, look me up.' He gave her his quick smile and, climbing into the Land-Rover, turned at a field entrance, and drove off.

By the time she drew up at the hotel, Janice had decided to ask about the job that evening.

After dinner, therefore, she asked the waitress if she might see Mr Murray. As she waited, she felt very nervous. In a

17

moment he appeared, a query expressed in his raised eyebrows.

'Miss Taylor? I hope everything is to your satisfaction.'

'Oh, yes, thank you,' Janice assured him. 'Actually, I'd like to talk to you about your advertisement.'

'My advertisement? About a house-keeper? I see. Would you come into my office please.'

Janice followed him in and took the seat which he indicated, feeling very like a schoolgirl called before the head-master.

He slowly explained what the job would involve. He needed someone to work with him in the management of the hotel, to organise the excellent working staff made up of local women. The bar, frequented all year by local residents, was staffed by a local couple who ran it between them. At the back of the hotel was a long building which had been partially converted to a bunk-type accommodation for parties of young people.

'My wife,' he explained in a level tone, 'was very keen on the idea, and

18

drew up the plans before her death last year. One of the new housekeeper's first jobs would be to decorate and equip the annexe in time for the ski-ing season.' He broke off, then asked:

'Do you have any qualifications?'

Janice explained about her course at Glasgow College of Domestic Science, and her experience in running the restaurant. She was able to produce from her handbag a glowing testimonial from the store manager.

As Hugh Murray read it, his brows drew together and he looked disappointed. He considered Janice without speaking for a moment, then shook his head.

'I'm afraid the job I have to offer wouldn't suit you, Miss Taylor,' he pronounced. 'I see by this that you're highly qualified, and extremely capable and efficient. Apart from the fact that the salary I'd offer couldn't interest you, I feel that you wouldn't have enough scope for your talents here.' He paused and rose, turning away from Janice as he spoke.

'You see, the most important part of

your job here wouldn't be the running of the hotel. It would be trying to provide something like a home atmosphere for my children. They need someone to care for them. Oh, I do my best, but with children it takes a woman's touch.' He swung round to face her. 'High qualifications don't necessarily equip a person for these duties, Miss Taylor.'

'No, Mr Murray.' Janice matched his cold tone. 'But neither do they disqualify me, surely?' She produced a second testimonial from her handbag. It was from the mother of four children whom Janice had looked after during College holidays one year. It told of the warm relationship which Janice had built up between herself and the children and of her patience and good nature with them.

'As for salary,' continued Janice, beginning to enjoy herself, 'surely it's for me to decide if it's adequate, if you decide to offer me the job. And surely that depends,' she rushed on, as he seemed about to interrupt, 'on whether the children take to me, and I to them!'

There was a pause as they looked rather warily at one another. Then Hugh

Murray smiled.

'I suggest that you stay here for a few days as my guest. Then, if things work out, I'll be happy to offer you the job. Are you free to stay?'

'Yes, I'm absolutely free,' Janice assured him.

And so, during the next few days, Janice came to know the Murray children.

Mary and Paul were eight-year-old twins, and Robbie was nearly five. Mary and Paul were physically alike, with their father's dark hair and eyes, but their natures were poles apart. Paul was a mischievous outgoing boy, already very interested in a man's world of fishing, cars and sport, while Mary was a quiet, restrained little girl with a rather worried and burdened expression. Robbie, though, with his shock of fair hair and his chubby cheeks, was a complete charmer.

On the second day, Hugh Murray suggested that Janice should go to meet the children from school. As she drove up to the school buildings, she was aware of curious glances from the occupants of various cars also awaiting children. After the other cars began to move away, there was still no sign of the Murray children, so Janice went to the door of the school. She heard Robbie's voice talking animatedly, and she hesitated at the classroom door.

The children were grouped round a table with an attractive young woman, who looked up and smiled at Janice, while Robbie hurried up to her, took her hand and drew her towards the table.

'Hello, Miss Janice! Come and look at my Guy Fawkes picture. I made it all myself. At least...' He glanced appealingly at his teacher. 'Miss Dawson helped me a little.'

'Just a very little, Robbie,' she assured him. 'You did splendidly.'

Janice admired the picture, and the children went to collect their outdoor things from the cloakroom.

'You must be Miss Taylor,' said the teacher. 'I'm Isobel Dawson. The children were telling me you're a special visitor.' Her look was frankly curious.

Janice was wondering how to reply when the children returned, and saved her from saying anything but a pleasant goodbye.

They returned to a welcome afternoon tea which the children ate hungrily, and the boys chatted freely to Janice and Mrs Mackay about their day at school, frequently referring to Miss Dawson, of whom they were obviously very fond. Mary spoke very little and watched Robbie constantly. She tried to spread his scone for him till he protested that he could do it himself.

'Are you coming to help with the bonfire, Miss Janice?' asked Paul. 'We're finishing it this afternoon, and we need some more branches to make it really enormous!'

'Where is it?' asked Janice.

'Just over in Mr Mackay's field, by the burn.'

'Can I come, too?' asked a voice. And there stood Hugh Murray—a different Hugh Murray from the one who had interviewed Janice. The lines of his face had softened as he smiled at his family.

Ten minutes later they set out to make the most of the remaining daylight. For a while they worked hard, cutting gorse and scrub, dragging it on to the already large pile.

'We've made a guy at school!' Paul informed them.

'Yes,' Robbie agreed, 'and it's got the horriblest face you've ever seen!'

Hugh Murray threw a large branch to the top of the pile and then rubbed his hands together.

'Well,' he said, 'it's getting late. We'd better head for home.'

They set off towards the hotel. Paul and Mary began to sing a song they had learned at school and Robbie joined in with more volume than tune.

'I used to know that!' exclaimed Janice, and joined in the next verse.

During the chorus, they were joined, to Janice's surprise, by Hugh Murray. Altogether, it was a merry company who tramped through the frosty dusk towards the welcoming lights of home.

Later it was homework time.

Paul and Mary read their pages fluently, and with expression.

'Now me, Miss Janice!' Robbie eagerly thrust his book at her.

'But I always hear your reading,

24

Robbie,' Mary protested anxiously.

'I want Miss Janice!' Robbie said determinedly.

Mary turned away and fiddled with her schoolbag, but not before Janice had noticed the look of resentment directed towards herself.

Mary's attitude was the only thing which made Janice wonder about staying at Kirkton. She liked the hotel and the district, and would enjoy the opportunity of ski-ing again. The boys seemed to like and accept her, Paul in a casual manner, but Robbie more demonstratively. It was this affection shown by Robbie which was causing Mary to withdraw more and more into herself.

CHAPTER 2

That evening, after the children were in bed, Hugh Murray joined Janice in the Resident's Lounge. This time, it was he who looked uncertain as he faced her.

'I was wondering,' he started, 'if you've decided whether or not you'll stay. I hope you will,' he added. 'I think you fit in here very well.'

Janice replied with equal frankness:

'I like it here very much. I like the district, and the way the hotel is run with such happy staff relations. Most important, I find your children interesting and—loveable.' She paused.

'Then you'll stay?' His voice was eager.

'Well I may as well be honest. I have one doubt about it, Mr Murray, and that concerns Mary. She obviously resents me, and to have me here permanently might make her very unhappy. It's nothing I've done or said to her, I know. In fact, I don't think it's personal at all. It's just that she'd resent anyone to whom Robbie shows affection.'

Hugh Murray sighed.

'Mary is a problem. Oh, not that she causes trouble. She's almost too good all the time. But she still cries at night and she won't let Robbie out of her sight.

'Have you tried talking to her about it?'

'Yes. But she just clams up and says that nothing's worrying her and that she's perfectly happy. I had Dr Macpherson have a look at her but he says it's just a matter of time.' He broke off and, rising, looked searchingly at Janice. 'Will you stay and give it a try?'

'I'll be happy to,' answered Janice and in an involuntary gesture her hand went out to him and was clasped firmly in his.

'Now, to talk business,' he began, and once more became the impersonal employer.

The next day, Saturday, was the fifth of November, and as Janice had

27

promised the children she'd be at the bonfire, she intended returning to Glasgow on the Sunday. She thought it would take her a week to complete her business there, and arrange for the flat to be let, furnished. While she was in Glasgow, she'd order all that was needed for the hotel annexe. Hugh Murray had given her a free hand within the limits on which they had agreed the previous evening.

Before lunch, Janice went to find Mary and found her playing with a doll's house, while the boys lined up soldiers round their toy fort.

'Mary,' said Janice. 'Would you like to come to the annexe with me and help me decide which colours to choose?'

'No, thank you,' replied Mary politely. Feeling suitably squashed, Janice went by herself.

The annexe contained two large, bright rooms which could each accommodate eight, in two-tier bunk beds. In addition, there were two small bedrooms which would do for the teacher or club leader. There were ample shower and toilet facilities and there was a large drying-room.

Janice spent a happy hour measuring and planning, and jotted down a few ideas.

That afternoon, while Hugh Murray was away with the children collecting the fireworks, Janice stayed behind to hold the fort. She went into the kitchen where Mrs Mackay was preparing a huge dish of stovies which would be carried over to the bonfire later that evening.

Hugh Murray had told the staff just that morning of Janice's decision to stay and Mrs Mackay greeted her with a smile.

'I hear you're coming to join us, Miss Taylor.'

'Yes, I'm going down to Glasgow tomorrow, but I'll be back by the middle of the month, to get settled in before the busy season.'

'That's just fine,' said Annie Mackay. 'These bairns need a woman around them. Especially Mary,' she added unexpectedly.

'Do you think so? She's the one I feel uncertain about. She seems to resent me.' Janice felt she could confide in this motherly woman.

'Mary's a quiet one,' the cook went on, 'and there's something she's not telling. There's something that bothers her about her mother.

'You'll be thinking I'm havering,' she added apologetically, 'but I've a feeling that she's needing to talk about it, but can't.'

'Perhaps you're right,' said Janice slowly. 'It's this complete obsession with Robbie that worries me.'

Mrs Mackay heaved the pot on to the cooker, and switched it on for their meal.

'It's queer,' she said. 'Mary never used to bother much about Robbie. Paul and she were thick as thieves, being twins. It's just that since the accident she's been like this.'

'Well, I can't see her confiding in me, the way things are at present,' Janice said gloomily.

Mrs Mackay looked at her, and smiled.

'Do you want me to show you around the kitchen and stores while we're not busy?'

She and Janice spent a profitable half

hour, and Janice remarked in surprise on the large stock of food in the deep freeze.

'Ay,' answered Annie. 'You've got to be prepared up here. If you're snowed in with a houseful of guests, it's amazing how quickly the food disappears!'

'But I thought, with the snow-ploughs...'

'Oh, they're very fine for the Glen road. But it's the last mile up to the hotel that's the trouble. There's a wee bit between the two bad bends the plough doesn't dare risk sometimes.'

'Oh, well,' remarked Janice. 'No cause for worry. We could stand a siege with what's in there!'

A thought came to her.

'Talking of the Glen road, is that a new hotel about a mile-up?'

'Ay, I'm afraid so,' Annie's expression darkened.

'Do you think it will harm trade here?'

'Ay, it could well do that, being on the main road. Well, Miss Taylor,' she added taking off her overall, 'I'll be off. Ye ken where everything is.'

Janice busied herself preparing a tea for the family, and when preparations were complete she went upstairs and changed into warm clothes to wear to the bonfire. As she combed her blonde hair, she couldn't help being pleased with her reflection in the mirror. She had some colour in her cheeks again and the look of strain had disappeared from around her blue eyes.

After tea, a chattering, laughing, warmly-clad group collected at the bonfire, armed with lanterns and torches. The guy, who did indeed have 'the horriblest face,' sat drunkenly on top. The fireworks were supervised by Donald Mackay, and kept at a safe distance.

The bonfire was an annual event in the Glen, and families from all around were there, children's faces, bright with expectancy, fathers organising with ill-concealed enthusiasm, and mothers enjoying their families' pleasure with just a little anxiety. Even Mary was smiling. She had insisted that she alone was to look after Robbie that evening, and was holding his hand, warning him frequently to 'be careful' and 'stand back.' Janice had agreed, knowing that if she did not, the evening would be spoiled for Mary, but she stayed close by as unobtrusively as possible.

As Hugh Murray lit the bonfire, a great cheer went up. Red flames leapt higher and branches crackled and sparked. There were cries of pleasure as Roman Candles flared.

As the fire took hold, the flames licked Guy Fawkes's legs, faces glowed in the dancing light.

Mary's face, Janice noticed, was more animated than she'd ever seen it. As for Robbie, he was wide-eyed and, for once, speechless, as Guy Fawkes collapsed in a spray of sparks.

When the fire had faded a little to a rosy glow, everyone enjoyed a steaming plate of Annie's delicious stovies. Attention then turned to the showier fireworks, and rockets lit the sky.

'So you're staying in the district, Miss Taylor?' said a voice, and Janice turned to see Isobel Dawson. As Janice replied, she noticed the schoolteacher's companion. It was Sandy Nicol, the vet, and he was smiling at her with unconcealed pleasure.

33

Isobel continued:

'You must come to the schoolhouse for supper one evening.' She turned to her companion, laying a hand on his arm with a proprietary air. 'Sandy, this is Miss Taylor,' she began, but Sandy broke in.

'We've already met. Hello again. So you changed your mind?'

Janice noted a fleeting look of annoyance on Isobel's face as she made to reply, when suddenly there was a loud bang, shouts of 'Look out!' and a child's terrified scream.

Turning back in horror towards the children, Janice saw Robbie, who had wandered away a few paces, clutching his head and screaming in terror. Smoke haloed his head.

'Help me! Daddy! Daddy!' he yelled, and went stumbling off, into the dark night.

In the split second that followed, Janice was aware of Hugh Murray's cold, accusing glance before he grabbed up a lantern, and set off after the terrified child.

In the confusion of screams and voices

which followed, Janice stood for a moment, numbed by shock and by a feeling of guilt at not being with the children.

These thoughts took only a moment to flash through her brain and were swiftly followed by a need for action.

'Look after Mary and Paul, please,' she said hurriedly to Isobel Dawson, and, turning, she ran, stumbling a little on the rough ground, to Hugh Murray's lantern.

She reached them just as Hugh seemed to rip off Robbie's dufflecoat in one powerful movement.

'Hold the lantern here,' he told Janice, 'till I have a look at him.'

Sick with apprehension, Janice did as she was told. Robbie was clinging to his father, sobbing and shuddering, as the surprisingly gentle hands made a quick examination.

Janice heard Hugh Murray breathe a deep sigh of relief as he straightened up.

'He's not badly hurt,' he told the few people who had gathered round.

He swung Robbie up into his arms and set off to the clear stream, with Janice almost trotting beside them with the lantern. She felt almost giddy with relief when they discovered that Robbie's injuries were not as serious as they'd first thought.

Carefully, Hugh Murray bathed the tender area of the child's skin, over and over again with the icy-cold water.

'That should take the heat out of it,' he said. 'Better now, Robbie?'

Robbie, his face bent over the burn and his hair dripping with water, answered through chittering teeth.

'I think I'm fine now, Dad. But I'm awfully cold.'

There was a general air of relief, and people began to disperse. Sandy Nicol appeared at Janice's side as Hugh Murray mopped Robbie's hair and wrapped him in his own warm jacket.

'Here's Robbie's coat,' said Sandy. 'The hood's damaged a bit. A spark must have shot out from the embers. It got caught in the folds of Robbie's hood.'

Janice shivered at the thought of what could have happened.

'I should never have turned away from

him,' she said miserably.

'Oh, it all happened so suddenly, you wouldn't have had time to prevent it,' Sandy told Janice comfortingly. 'All the fireworks were under supervision, of course, but no-one could have foreseen an accident as a result of a spark.'

Janice felt someone tug impatiently at her sleeve. It was Paul.

'Come quickly, Miss Janice,' he whispered urgently. 'There's something wrong with Mary.'

Janice followed him quickly. Mary was crying her heart out, while Isobel Dawson tried to comfort her.

'I can't understand what's wrong with her,' the teacher said despairingly.

Mary continued sobbing as Janice put an arm around her shoulders.

'Come on, Mary,' she said, 'Let's go home. Robbie's all right now, but we all need a nice, warm drink.'

It was a strange ending to the festive evening as the small party set off back to the hotel. Hugh Murray carried Robbie, while Janice led Mary, who still sobbed in a heart-broken manner and couldn't be comforted.

'It's my fault. It's my fault,' she was saying through her sobs, and Janice found an echo to these words in her own heart. She couldn't forget the accusation in Hugh Murray's eyes, and she blamed herself bitterly for what had happened.

Dr Macpherson dressed Robbie's injury, and gave both Robbie and Mary a light sedative. Soon the three children were tucked up in bed, and Janice left them in the dimly-lit bedroom, hoping that sleep would come quickly.

She went to the kitchen to prepare sandwiches and coffee for everyone who had returned to the hotel after the bonfire, and was piling the sandwiches on to plates when Hugh Murray entered. His face was expressionless and, as Janice glanced at him, the words of apology died before reaching her lips.

'I'll take these through,' he said, civilly enough, 'if you bring the coffee when it's ready.'

'Very well,' replied Janice. 'Then I'll slip up to see if the children are asleep yet.'

When she opened the door of the children's bedroom. Janice saw that Paul and Robbie were sound asleep, but in the dim light she could see Mary's eyes were wide open, and the little girl was lying stiff and straight in her bed.

'Can't you get to sleep?' whispered Janice.

Mary shook her head wordlessly and large tears welled, silently trickling down the sides of her face. Janice sat down on the bed and took Mary's hand.

'Can't you tell me what's the matter?' she asked gently. 'Robbie's all right now, you know. So what's worrying you so much?'

'It was my fault,' said Mary desperately. 'I wasn't watching him. I have to, you see. I have to look after him all the time. And I watched the fireworks instead. It was my fault.'

'It was my fault too, Mary,' said Janice softly. 'It's my job to look after all of you. That's why I'm here.'

'But it's different for me. I promised I'd look after him.' The weary hopelessness in her voice was worse than sobbing. Then, as Janice talked on, soothingly and reassuringly, the sedative began taking effect. Slowly, the heavy eyelids

39

drooped, and the tense little body relaxed into sleep.

Janice slipped out of the room and went to join the company in the lounge. As she entered the room and Hugh Murray introduced her to everyone, mostly people from the Glen, Janice was most aware of the friendliness they showed towards her, and she felt herself relaxing in the welcoming atmosphere. Hugh Murray was a charming host and no hint of tension affected his pleasant manner.

Eventually, everyone except Sandy and Isobel Dawson had left. They were on first name-terms with Hugh Murray and it was natural that Janice should be so with them. She found this came easily with Sandy and Isobel, but she carefully avoided addressing Hugh by name. He seemed to feel the same constraint.

'You must come to supper at the school-house, Janice,' Isobel invited. 'When would it suit?'

'Well, I plan to go to Glasgow tomorrow for a few days,' replied Janice. 'I'm making the arrangements for letting my flat, and doing some shopping for the ski-annexe. But I should be back by the weekend.'

'I'll phone you,' nodded Isobel.

'How is Glasgow these days?' enquired Sandy. 'I haven't been down for months. I spent my student days there.'

'It changes so fast I can't keep up,' replied Janice. 'Every week another landmark seems to disappear. Talking about student days, I always enjoyed those dances at Vet College.'

'Did you really go to them? That would be after my time, of course!' Sandy replied laughingly.

Quite oblivious of the other two, Janice and Sandy began to reminisce about their student days. Both had frequented the same coffee bars, patronised the same little cinema off Sauchiehall Street and eaten the same, filling spaghetti dishes in a favourite Italian restaurant. Sandy had been in his last year at college during Janice's first year at 'Dough School.' This seemed a wonderful coincidence, to them and they were at the "Did you know so-and-so?" stage, when Janice suddenly remembered

41

the other two. Hugh was staring at his cup, while Isobel fidgeted impatiently with her handbag.

'Oh, dear,' said Janice contritely, 'I didn't realise we were being so rude. Nothing's more boring than other people's reminiscences!'

The conversation became general again, and soon Isobel rose to go home. Sandy had brought her in the Land-Rover, and as they all went to the front door to say goodnight, Sandy spoke quietly to Janice.

'You're going to Glasgow tomorrow? I may be down next week on business. Perhaps we could have dinner?'

Janice felt a surge of pleasure and she gave him the telephone number of her Glasgow flat.

Meanwhile, Hugh was helping Isobel into the Land-Rover. Janice had noticed that they didn't have much to say to each other, and Hugh was always a little formal and restrained with Isobel, as she was with him.

After the Land-Rover was out of sight, Janice emptied the ash-trays and cleared away, while Hugh locked up. They were both very tired now and there was little conversation. When everything was tidy, Janice slowly made her way upstairs to look in on the children. At the door of their room she encountered Hugh Murray. Too tired for pretence, she briefly said:

'I'm sorry. I should have been watching Robbie.'

He looked at her for a few seconds and she saw that he, too, looked exhausted.

'It wouldn't have made much difference,' he answered wearily. 'It all happened so quickly.' He turned to enter the children's room, then paused.

'Goodnight, Janice,' he said.

'Goodnight, Hugh.'

Janice lay for some time that night before she could sleep. So much had happened since the morning that her mind was in a turmoil. She had started the day full of confidence that she could cope with this family, and help to provide the security that the children needed. Now, in one careless moment, she had failed to prevent harm coming to Robbie, had worsened Mary's anxiety, and had shaken Hugh Murray's confidence in her capability.

Resolutely she turned her mind to more soothing thoughts, remembering Sandy's dinner invitation. The look in his eyes was not cold and accusing, like Hugh Murray's, but warm with admiration. Thinking of Sandy, she at last drifted into sleep.

CHAPTER 3

Janice left for Glasgow the following morning after noticing how Robbie appeared to have fully recovered from his mishap, while Mary was still brooding.

The roads were quiet and she made good time. As her car soared over a new motorway fly-over, she caught sight of Glasgow's ancient cathedral, backed by a skyline of old and new, merging in a strange compatibility. Perhaps, she thought, the new city will, after all, be beautiful.

Soon after midday, she reached the flat. The empty rooms seemed unwelcoming, and Janice shivered a little as she entered. With the electric fire flickering, however, and a snack prepared on a tray, she felt much more cheerful. As she ate, she planned which things she'd leave in the flat, which articles should be stored, and which personal odds and ends she'd take back to Kirkton with her.

All afternoon and evening she worked, packing things away, and was glad to have a warm, relaxing bath before dropping into bed.

Monday was taken up with business. She visited her solicitor who came to view the flat in the afternoon, and who assured her that its central position and comfortable fittings would ensure a speedy let.

On Tuesday morning she visited a large Buchanan Street store, where she chose the curtains, quilt fabric and carpets for the annexe of the hotel. When she completed her purchases, Janice felt as though she'd done a good morning's work, and left the store for a breath of air before lunch.

She was walking along Buchanan Street when she came face to face with a young man. As he approached, his face broke into a smile of pleased recognition.

'Janice Taylor!' he exclaimed. 'How are you?'

'Jack! I'm very well, thank you. How about you? You look just the same.'

'And you too! Where are you going? I'm just going for some lunch. Would you care to join me?'

Janice soon found herself sitting opposite this old friend from her college days. At that time he had been a Physical Education student. Now, at twenty-seven, he was head of his department in a city school.

'I've just been ordering some ski-equipment,' he explained. 'It's the latest sport to be added to the list of choices. It's great what the kids get nowadays. When I was at school it was rounders or nothing!

'But enough of me.' Jack smiled. 'What have you been doing with yourself? Not married yet?' He nodded at her ringless left hand.

Janice briefly told him what she'd been doing since she last saw him. He was very interested to hear about the new ski-annexe at Kirkton House Hotel, and made a note of the address in his diary.

'I can't promise,' he said as he put his diary away, 'but I'm almost sure you've made your first booking. I'll see you in the New Year, complete with party of school kids, always supposing that Margaret will let me go!'

Without much persuasion, he produced a photo of his fair, pretty wife, Margaret, and their blond, baby son.

It was altogether a very pleasant encounter, and they parted after lunch in good spirits.

In the afternoon, Janice bought clothes, for the children, who needed new outfits for the parties they'd attend over Christmas time.

By the time she reached home Janice was looking forward to washing her hair and watching television.

Before she settled down to a quiet evening though, she had to phone Kirkton to tell Hugh Murray about the materials and colours she'd chosen, so that he could make the arrangements with the painters.

Hugh sounded very businesslike on the phone as they discussed the colour schemes.

'How is Robbie now?' Janice enquired.

'He's much better now. The pain has gone completely.'

'And Mary?'

Hugh's tone changed.

'She's very withdrawn, I'm afraid. She seeems to feel guilty about the accident.'

Janice was silent.

'Well,' he added briskly, 'when will you be back?'

'I'll come up on Friday afternoon,' answered Janice. 'I'm showing some people over the flat on Thursday.'

With this, the conversation ended, and Janice, feeling rather deflated went through to wash her hair.

She was just working up a rich lather again when the phone rang.

'Blast!' she said. After wrapping a towel round her head, she went to answer. She gave her number in a rather bad-tempered voice, as water was trickling down her neck, and lather was nipping her eyes.

'Hello,' said a man's voice. 'Janice?'

'Yes. Who's that?'

'Sandy. You don't sound like your usual sweet self, somehow.'

'Well, just you try standing there with

shampoo in your eyes and water running down the back of your neck, and see how you sound!' said Janice, wrathfully.

'Oh, dear. An awkward moment? Sorry.'

There was a click as he rang off, and Janice was left staring in disbelief at the mouth piece.

'Well, of all the...!' She began, and she marched back to the bathroom in a fury. Then she began to laugh ruefully, reflecting that it was just what she deserved. She lathered up her hair again, and turned on the water to rinse, but suddenly it occured to her that she might not hear the phone when Sandy rang back. Grabbing her towel again, she ran to open the sitting-room door and returned, leaving the bathroom door ajar.

He hadn't rung by the time she finished washing her hair, nor by the time she set it in large rollers. She switched her hair dryer on, and had just settled down with it, when she realised that it, too, might drown the sound of the phone and so promptly switched it off again.

This is ridiculous! she told herself.

Surely Sandy Nicol isn't all that important to me!

By nine o'clock, Janice's hair had been dried by the heat of the electric fire, but Sandy still hadn't rung. She watched television for an hour, then feeling rather depressed, went to switch on the kettle, and toast some bread for supper.

It was then that the phone rang.

Janice hurried through and snatched up the receiver.

'Hello,' she said breathlessly. 'Sandy?'

'Please, is this the residence of Miss Taylor?' said the voice with a heavy, mid-European accent.

'Oh, yes. Sorry!' said a horrified Janice. 'Who is speaking, please?'

'Here speaks Herr Rauchman. Have you to let a furnished apartment?'

'Yes, that's right. But you'd have to contact my solicitor about it. His phone number is...'

But Janice was interrupted by a familiar laugh.

'Sandy!' she shrieked, 'you fool!'

'Well,' said Sandy, 'I didn't get a very friendly reception last time. Just thought I'd try a different attitude.'

51

'I am sorry about the other phone call,' Janice apologised.

'Well, I'll tell you how to make amends. Have dinner with me tomorrow. I'm coming down to Glasgow on business.'

'I'd like that very much,' said Janice. She gave him directions to the flat, and he arranged to pick her up at eight o'clock.

When Janice replaced the receiver, she stood for a moment, lost in happy thought.

It was only when the smell of burning toast came wafting through from the kitchen that she remembered her supper. A mixture of black smoke and belching steam met her at the kitchen door.

'This man,' said Janice wryly to herself, as she flung the kitchen window wide, 'has the most drastic effect on my efficiency!'

CHAPTER 4

Wednesday was spent tying up various loose ends, and Janice had a busy day finalising arrangements with her solicitor and bank manager, but by eight o'clock, she was dressed and ready for Sandy to appear.

She'd decided to wear her swirling skirt in black and white tweed topped by a black blouse. Her blonde hair was highlighted by the dark colours and the whole effect was striking.

Promptly at eight o'clock, the doorbell rang. Janice took a deep breath and walked calmly to the door. On opening it she saw a much more elegant Sandy than the one she was used to seeing up in Perthshire.

'Hello, Sandy,' said Janice, and in spite of herself she couldn't help adding,

'You do look smart!'

'Did you expect the old tweed jacket and welly boots?' grinned Sandy. 'Taking of looks, you look quite breathtaking yourself. I've booked a table at this new Garbrooke Hotel for eightthirty. Unfortunately though, I'll have to leave fairly early as I've to drive home tonight, to be in time for an appointment early tomorrow.'

'I shan't be a moment,' said Janice. 'I'll just get my coat.' As she went to the bedroom, she reflected that, however nervous she was before an encounter with Sandy, somehow his actual presence dispelled all her tension. She might have known him forever.

They had a delicious meal at the Garbrooke, and Janice had never tasted a more tender steak.

Throughout their meal, she and Sandy chatted. First they reminisced about their student days and shared memories of Glasgow as it used to be. Then Sandy told her of his childhood, spent in the Glen where his widowed father was still gamekeeper on one of the large estates; of his married sister, living in London, and of the other vet with whom he shared a cottage in Blairochry.

Janice, for her part, had resolved not to mention Isobel Dawson, but couldn't help wondering about her relationship with Sandy. They seemed to know each other so well. Now she found herself asking:

'Did Isobel Dawson grow up in the Glen, too?'

'Oh, yes,' said Sandy. He looked surprised for a second, then added. 'But you won't know about Isobel.' He paused. 'She was brought up at Kirkton House. Where the hotel is now.'

'Oh!' said Janice, in surprise. She had not, it seemed, been imagining the strain between Isobel and Hugh Murray. Sandy was frowning at his plate.

'The house belonged to Isobel's father's family. He inherited it with the family business. Then he went through all the money. He didn't have a head for business, and finally even the house had to go. On the morning of the sale, Isobel's father took a stroke, and died the following week.'

'How awful,' whispered Janice.

'Yes. Mrs Dawson has never really recovered. She has something of an obsession about it. She gave Isobel no peace till she took a job in the district. She's an unusual woman—but you'll meet her when you go to supper at the schoolhouse.'

Just then, a trolley laden with delicious-looking trifles and gateaux arrived at their table, and the subject was changed.

Some time later, over coffee, Sandy enquired:

'Do you think you'll like life in the Glen? It's quite a change from Glasgow and London.'

'I'm sure I shall,' answered Janice. 'The people seem so friendly. And my job should be interesting—when I start real work! So far, it's been a hotel without guests.'

'That should soon be remedied. Kirkton House is busy most of the year. It's only at this time there's nothing doing. At least,' Sandy frowned and continued slowly, 'that's how it was up till the accident, when Hugh's wife was killed. Hugh closed the place for a month after that, cancelled all the Christmas and

56

New Year bookings. It could take a while to build them up again.'

'What about the new hotel that's being built?'

Sandy shrugged.

'Who knows? It could be difficult, especially at first. People like to visit somewhere new. I think Hugh's quite worried about it.'

'Is it owned by local people?'

'No. It's some foreign group. Quite a big concern.'

'I seem to do nothing but ask questions,' said Janice apologetically.

'And I haven't talked so much for years. We've been very solemn, and I like to see you smile. Come.' He rose and stretched out a hand. 'Let's dance.'

He led her to the small dance floor where a few couples were dancing. The music was slow and Janice felt more relaxed than she had done for months.

'I hate to say it,' said Sandy presently, 'but I must go soon. It's quite a drive back and I have an early appointment in the morning.'

They drove back to Janice's flat, and he saw her to the door. She opened it, then turned to face him before going in to the flat.

'I won't ask you in,' she said, 'as I know you're anxious to be on your way. I've had a lovely evening, Sandy.'

He put his arms around her and hugged her close for a moment. Then he kissed her gently on the lips.

'I'll see you soon. Goodnight, Janice.' He was gone.

Next day, Thursday, Janice was kept busy showing the flat to people sent by her solicitor. She was surprised how her role as prospective landlady affected her attitude.

A young couple, who were both doing research at the University, would normally have appealed to her, with their informal, friendly manners. Now she noticed their feckless attitude, suspecting that they had minds above such things as housework. A middle-aged couple, who were to be in Glasgow for a year on business, seemed much more promising tenants.

When the last of the viewers had gone, Janice was able to confirm with her solicitor that the business couple were eager to have the flat at the agreed rent, and would move in the following week.

Before Janice left the flat on Friday, she had a last walk round it, taking everything in. This was where she had spent her childhood and grown up, the only home she had ever had, a haven of understanding where she was always welcome. But now, without the loving presence of her mother, it was home no longer. She must make her own.

Before she had time to be sentimental, Janice packed the car with the bits and pieces she was taking to her hotel room, and after locking up, set off for Kirkton.

Driving up the Stirling road, she thought of the last time she had passed this way. She had been full of doubts about the wisdom of her plans. Now, she could allow herself no doubts, and no looking back.

She reached Blairochry around three o'clock and stopped for petrol at the Riverside Garage. A large foreign car was parked in the forecourt. The bonnet of the car was open and beside it stood the driver, in conversation with the mechanic and the garage owner. No-one noticed Janice, and after a few minutes she got out of the car.

The driver of the other car was immaculately dressed, and Janice guessed by his accent that he was not British.

'But it is ridiculous!' he was protesting. 'Why do you not have this spare part?'

'Well, it's like this, sir,' explained the mechanic slowly, 'we don't get that many cars like this around these parts. There's no agent this side of Dundee.'

'What, then, can be done?'

'Well,' broke in the garage owner, 'I'll phone Dundee, and ask them to get this spare on the bus right away. If Dave's willing to put in a bit of overtime, we might have the car back on the road tomorrow.'

'That's all very well,' said the stranger, 'but what to do now? I am a very busy man and I have an important business meeting. Already I am late.'

He extracted a card from his wallet.

'My business is with Mr Hugh Murray, Kirkton House Hotel. Do you know this place?'

Janice, startled at hearing Hugh Murray's name, glanced over at the
60

stranger. What business could he have with Hugh? He certainly didn't look like any of the sales representatives who called at the hotel on business.

Just then the garage owner bustled over, full of apology, and attended to Janice. As he filled her tank, he continued his discussion with the stranger, and Janice was a very interested bystander. Seemingly, the two cars available for hire from the garage were out for the weekend, and the taxi was on a trip to Perth, and wasn't due back for at least an hour.

'But that is too long to wait!' protested the man. 'Is there no other way?'

'Excuse me,' said Janice. 'I could take you to Kirkton House, if that would solve your problem.'

The man swung to face her, seeming to notice her for the first time.

'Excellent!' he said. He turned to the garage owner. 'Send your taxi up to Kirkton House Hotel immediately it returns,' he instructed, 'I shall require it for the rest of the day.'

Janice paid for her petrol and got into her car.

As the back seat of the mini was covered with various odds and ends which she'd brought up from Glasgow, she leaned over to open the front door for her passenger.

When he had collected a briefcase from his own car, he settled himself into the passenger seat, saying:

'But I have not yet introduced myself. I am Johann Traub. I am from Zurich in Switzerland and I have come to Scotland on business.'

'I'm Janice Taylor.'

After they shook hands, Janice started the engine and headed across the river and up the Glen Road.

'Is this your first visit to Scotland?' she enquired.

'Indeed, no. I have been over many times to this area. I have business interests here. I find the countryside most pleasant, and the climate most invigorating.'

'And so is your country,' answered Janice. 'I spent a winter holiday in Lucerne three years ago.'

They conversed politely in this way for some miles.

'I hope I do not take you out of your way?' enquired Herr Traub.

Janice smiled.

'I believe we have the same destination. Kirkton House Hotel.'

'You are on holiday at this hotel?'

'No. I am house-keeper there.'

'So? Have you been working there long?'

Janice explained that she had come only very recently, and briefly mentioned her previous job in London.

'How many persons do you have working at the hotel?' was Herr Traub's next question.

Something in his tone told Janice that this had become more than polite conversation. This man was most interested in her answers. Suddenly, she thought she knew the nature of his business in this area. Instead of answering his question, she asked one of him.

'Are you interested in the hotel trade then, Herr Traub?'

There was a pause, and her companion laughed shortly.

'I suspect you have found me out, Miss Taylor. Yes, my interests are in the hotel trade. In fact, my newest interest is in the hotel development in this Glen, as I think you have already guessed.'

Janice was disarmed by his frankness.

'It had occurred to me,' she admitted, smiling. 'When do you plan to open?'

'In three weeks, we hope.'

'Why did you decide to build a hotel in Scotland?' It was Janice's turn to ask questions.

'My associates and I believe that your country has great potential. It is relatively undeveloped, compared with Switzerland, and now that we are fellow Europeans, it seemed a good idea to invest a little in Scotland. Our hotel will be modern and cosmopolitan. There is need of such places in Scotland!'

When they reached the turn-off to Kirkton House Hotel, Janice had to concentrate on her driving as the road twisted upward. Her companion, too, seemed pre-occupied, and they did not speak again until the car stopped on the gravel outside the hotel entrance.

'Well, Miss Taylor,' said Herr Traub, as they entered the hotel together, 'I am most grateful to you. Perhaps we shall work together in the future...'

Janice could think of no answer to this surprising remark, and at that moment Hugh Murray appeared. She left the two men as they entered the office and hurried to the kitchen, where she knew the children would be having something to eat on their return from school. As she went, she wondered what Herr Traub could have meant by his parting words.

She received a warm welcome from Annie Mackay and the children. Robbie gave her an enthusiastic hug, Paul a cheerful grin, and even Mary produced a smile. Annie's welcome took the form of a cup of tea and a freshly-baked girdle scone, thick with butter.

When Jane took in the afternoon tea to Hugh Murray and Herr Traub, she couldn't help noticing that the papers on the table included a large ordnance survey map of the immediate area, with various marks boldly drawn on it with red pen. Her curiosity was really awakened, and she felt that change was in the air.

After Janice compiled the menu and

made advance preparations for dinner, she unpacked her car and carried her things to the room which would now be her home.

It was beside the children's room, along the back passage on the first floor. Though not very large, it had been furnished to serve as a bed-sitting room, and with her records and books installed, and a favourite print on the wall, Janice knew she would feel quite at home.

As she and the children brought the last parcel and the suitcase from the car, the taxi from Blairochry drew up. Janice was debating whether to interrupt the meeting to inform Herr Traub of its arrival, when the office door opened and the two men emerged. Herr Traub looked as cool as ever and was smiling blandly.

'Do not be hasty,' he told Hugh as they came out. 'Take time to consider, and I'm sure you'll come to the right decision.'

Hugh looked impassive as he shook hands with his visitor and bade him goodbye. Then Herr Traub turned to Janice, who was by her car.

'Goodbye, Miss Taylor,' he said as he entered the taxi. 'And thank you for all your help.' His door was closed and the taxi drove off.

Hugh Murray stepped forward and picked up Janice's suitcase.

'I'll take this up,' he said shortly. 'I want to talk to you.'

Janice handed the parcel to Mary.

'There are some new clothes for you three. Go to your room and try them for size. I'll be with you in a minute.'

The three ran off excitedly.

As Janice made her way to her room, she wondered what Hugh would tell her. She was certainly not prepared for the hostile reception she received from him.

'Just what,' he began ominously, 'were you telling Herr Traub about the hotel during your tête-à-tête on the way up?'

For a moment, Janice was speechless. She stared at Hugh, feeling herself flush with anger at his unwarranted attack. He, interpreting the blush as one of guilt, continued:

'I know you haven't been here long,

but I did expect more loyalty from you.'

Janice, having got her breath back, opened her mouth to protest but he went on quickly:

'I heard, you know. "Perhaps we'll be working together, Miss Taylor," and "Thank you for all your help, Miss Taylor." Well, I have news for you. I have no intention of giving in so easily, whatever you may think!'

He swung round and left the room, leaving Janice staring unbelievingly after him. To her immense chagrin, tears began to form in her eyes and she could do nothing to stop them. She sat down in a chair and covered her face with her hands, trying desperately to pull herself together.

It was the unfairness that hurt her most. She had been so careful not to discuss the hotel, and now she was being accused of gossiping about it to a complete stranger. Oh, how could Hugh Murray be so unjust?

As she sat there, the tears gradually lessened and anger took their place. How dare he talk to her as if she were a disobedient child!

She rose and went to the wash-basin, splashing her face with hot, then cold water, over and over again, to remove the tell-tale tear stains. As she patted her face dry on the towel, there was a knock at the door, and Paul's voice called.

'May we come in?'

Hastily Janice looked at her reflection in the mirror. It wasn't as bad as she'd feared, and she called the children to enter. As they trooped in, dressed in their new outfits which she had chosen, she felt her spirits lighten.

'Oh, you do look smart!' she cried.

They certainly did. Perhaps Paul's shirt-tail hung out and Robbie's tie had a most unconventional knot, but the colours and sizes were just right. Mary, in her delicate cream dress, her face a little flushed with pleasure, looked prettier than Janice had ever seen her.

'These are the nicest things we've had for ages, aren't they, Mary?' said Paul.

'Oh, yes,' agreed Mary. 'Thank you for getting them, Miss Janice. You chose just right!'

This, coming from such an unexpected quarter, nearly set Janice off again, but she managed to smile and, after admiring each individually, sent them back to change out of their new clothes before their meal.

She hastily brushed her hair and made her face presentable, before hurrying downstairs to the kitchen. Annie was just leaving, and Janice prepared the evening meal for the family. She was still angry with Hugh Murray, but as she knew that she was so definitely in the right, she decided to leave things for the moment. The family meal, therefore, passed un-eventfully, the children's chatter hiding the adults' silence.

After the meal, when the children had gone upstairs, and the dishes were stacked in the washer, Janice set about preparing dinner for the guests. Janice and Etta were kept working at top speed to serve everyone, and Janice was completing the grilling of Angus steaks when Hugh Murray appeared.

'There are two more guests for dinner. Can you cope?'

'Certainly,' answered Janice coolly.

For the next hour or so, there was little breathing space for either of them but, after coffee had been served, they flopped in the kitchen and enjoyed a much-needed cup themselves, before clearing up and setting the dishwasher to do its work. Etta, the waitress went to collect the coffee cups and returned, smiling.

'They all enjoyed their meal, at any rate,' she reported. 'The eight of them are away, but the other two are talking to Mr Murray just now. They're fair pleased.'

Janice felt pleased, too. This was the first real catering job she had been called upon to do at the hotel, and she was content that everything had gone well. At least Hugh couldn't find fault with her on this score!

When Etta had hurried off home, Janice stayed to tidy the kitchen. Hugh Murray entered and walked over to where she stood.

'Janice,' he began, but seemed unable to go on. Janice looked at him levelly. It was the first time she had seen him disconcerted.

'Janice,' he began again, and there was almost an appealing note in his voice,

'I believe I owe you an apology. I said some unjustified things to you this afternoon.'

'Yes,' agreed Janice calmly, 'you certainly did. Do you always jump to conclusions so quickly?'

Then, seeing him flinch a little, she knew what it was costing this reserved man to apologise, and she couldn't find it in her heart to make it any harder for him. In any case, a harder heart than hers would have found it difficult not to soften a little towards someone who suddenly looked so vulnerable. Her tone, therefore, was lighter as she continued:

'Do you really think I would go gossiping about your business affairs to a complete stranger?'

Heartened by the change of tone, Hugh answered eagerly.

'Not really. When I had time to think about it, it seemed impossible. I'm afraid I wasn't thinking very clearly this afternoon. The whole affair has really thrown me. But that's no excuse for taking it out on you, I'm very sorry.'

He did look contrite, and Janice smiled at him.

'It's all right, Hugh,' she said. 'But what DID Herr Traub say to you? Or am I not supposed to ask?'

'Indeed you must know. I'd like to talk it over with you, in fact. It would help me to clear my own mind. Are you finished in here?'

'Almost,' said Janice, 'but I'm hungry. You must be, too. Why not sit here at the table and tell me about it, while I make us something to eat?'

'Thank you. I could do with something if it's not too much trouble.' He seated himself at the end of the table.

Janice noticed that, apology over, his tone had resumed much of its usual businesslike tone. He was silent for a moment and then he began to talk, slowly, as if thinking the matter through as he spoke.

'When we took over Kirkton House to run it as a hotel, we—that is, my wife, Sheila, and I—had very definite ideas about what kind of place we wanted it to be. We tried to keep the "country house" atmosphere. We both felt the house had real character, which we didn't want to destroy. As you know, it's

73

not a huge place, but eight letting bedrooms were enough to run as a family business, without employing a large resident staff. We did quite well. People tended to come back year after year—people who like a quiet holiday—touring a bit and walking or fishing. Many of them came for a spring or autumn week which extended our season. They often said they liked the family atmosphere, and Sheila had a good way with them.'

He paused, and his hands played restlessly with the cutlery on the table in front of him. When he continued, his voice was flat.

'Then Sheila was killed. I suppose I didn't care much what happened to the hotel for a while after that. I cancelled all the bookings over last Christmas. During the rest of the year, some of our regulars came as usual. They hadn't heard about Sheila, and I think it put a damper on their whole stay here. I don't think they'll come back. People want to be carefree on holiday.'

He was quiet for a moment. Then he looked up at Janice, who was standing by the cooker, glad to have something to do. Sympathy was the last thing Hugh wanted from her at this time.

'So you see,' he continued expressionlessly, 'business hasn't been good. Of course, at the peak of the season we were busy as ever. Accommodation is at a premium round here in high summer and early autumn. But that's too short a season. The outlook isn't very bright at the moment, and it's at the same moment that Herr Traub arrives with his offer.'

Janice carefully set a large omelette before him, and poured his coffee.

'A good offer?' she ventured.

'An excellent offer.'

'Will you accept?'

'Can I afford not to?' he answered wryly. 'Herr Traub and his associates have made their proposition very attractive indeed. They want to buy me out—hotel, land, the lot. They've made me a generous offer, above market value, and have arranged that I can stay on as manager.'

'But why?' enquired Janice, puzzled. 'What do they want with Kirkton House when they've built that huge new hotel up the road?'

'That's what I wondered,' replied Hugh, 'and I think I know the answer. They're not interested in the house at all—it's the land they want. I have all the land up the hill at the back there. Donald Mackay has grazing rights for his sheep over some of it, but there's good shooting too. Then there's the loch at the top, with fine fishing. These would be real assets if they intend developing the area.'

'What are their plans for the house itself?'

'There's the rub,' said Hugh. 'Herr Traub was rather evasive on the subject, but I can't see a big concern like his being interested in keeping it in its present form. No, I suspect that Kirkton House Hotel would very shortly be phased out of their plans.'

Janice made an involuntary sound of protest. Hugh looked at her enquiringly.

'It would be such a pity,' she explained. 'There are so many of these faceless, cosmopolitan places going up everywhere—all looking the same and serving the same sort of food. Surely there's room for a hotel like this, with it's own atmosphere and good Scottish food. I'm sure people still want what we have to offer!'

Her heated tone surprised even herself, and Hugh surveyed her with raised eyebrows.

'I didn't know you felt so strongly about it,' he said.

Janice, feeling rather foolish, continued more calmly.

'Herr Traub told me that Scotland needed these new hotels, and I agree. But it also needs to hold on to its own character and style. That's what attracts tourists from England and overseas.'

Feeling that she had said enough, Janice rose and cleared the table. Hugh Murray also rose to his feet.

'I'll sleep on it,' he said wearily. 'It's too late to make sensible decisions tonight.' Then his tone changed. 'I almost forgot to tell you a piece of good news after all the gloom. The couple who came in late for dinner were so pleased with the meal and the hotel that they've booked the whole place over Christmas.

They're arranging a family reunion over the festive season with brothers and sisters coming with their families from all over. One's even coming from New Zealand!'

'Quite a clan gathering,' Janice smiled. 'That is good news.'

On this more cheerful note, they went their separate ways.

Janice had intended to tidy her bedroom that night, as there were things still lying on the bed and on chairs, but she was too exhausted, and, dumping the papers and boxes from the bed to the floor, she resolved to do it in the morning.

In the short time before she slept, she had a feeling that something was on her mind. It came to her as she drifted into sleep that she'd half expected that Sandy might phone.

CHAPTER 5

After breakfast the next morning, Janice went back to her room to make order out of chaos. Her clothes were already put away, and her records and books arranged, but there remained personal papers and letters, many of which came from her mother's writing desk, which she just couldn't throw away, but she had nowhere suitable to keep them. Finally, she decided to put them all in to a cardboard box and stow them in her wardrobe.

This task took much longer than she'd expected. She kept finding things from her past which could not be packed away without at least a look. Old photographs of herself, a plump toddler, a tomboy, a gawky schoolgirl, received a smiling glance. Others, taken on family holidays, brought back memories of summers long past, spent at Arran or

Girvan with her parents. One, taken on the promenade at Ayr, showed the three of them leaving the beach, damp hair and rolled towels witnessing that they'd been in the sea. She turned the snap over and there, written in her mother's hand was: *Janice swam three strokes today!* and the date.

Through the tears in her eyes, Janice stared at the writing, and in a flash recalled clearly a day so long forgotten. How patiently had her parents stood waist-deep in the chill Scottish sea, as she struggled to master her fear. How proud and happy they all were when she at last took courage to swim three strokes. Carefully, she replaced the snap with the rest, and laid them in the carton.

The next thing she came upon was a bundle of letters with London post-marks. The writing was bold and masculine and she instantly recognised it as being Bryan's. These were the letters he had written to her when she'd returned to nurse her mother in Glasgow.

She picked out the last one, the one she hadn't answered—it had come when nothing in the world mattered, but the care of her mother. It was a puzzled, hurt letter, unlike those which he had written previously. Janice felt contrite as she read it, but reminded herself that she had written again to him, after her mother's death, and that this time it was Bryan who had neglected to reply. His hurt had obviously healed quickly!

Glancing at her watch, Janice was appalled to see how much time she had idled away. Quickly, she piled all the other papers into the box and shut it in her wardrobe. Running downstairs, her thoughts returned to Bryan. It was the first time she had thought of him in weeks. Her thoughts were now for someone else. Perhaps Bryan's hurt had healed quickly, but so, to be fair, had her own.

Perhaps Sandy will phone tonight, she thought.

It was after lunch, when Janice was clearing the table, that Paul called her.

'There's a phone call for you,' he said.

Janice hurried to the phone in anticipation, but the voice at the other end couldn't be Sandy, not even in disguise. It was distinctly feminine and belonged to Isobel Dawson. She was phoning as promised to invite Janice to supper at the schoolhouse. They fixed it for Wednesday evening.

'Did you enjoy your visit to Glasgow?' enquired Isobel.

'Yes, thanks, though most of it was pretty busy,' Janice answered.

'Yes, so Sandy was telling me. Well, see you on Wednesday. Just come when you can.'

As she rang off, Janice felt rather uncomfortable. Sandy certainly seemed to spend a great deal of time in Isobel's company.

She walked back through to the kitchen, deep in thought. Annie Mackay was finishing a cup of tea, the daily paper spread out in front of her.

'Och, it's Miss Dawson!' she suddenly exclaimed. 'Look, isn't she bonnie in that dress?'

Janice looked over her shoulder at the photograph.

'Some guests at the Blairochry Farmers' Dance,' ran the caption, and there was Isobel, looking very pretty indeed, on the arm of Sandy Nicol.

Janice felt a painful pang of jealousy, and also shame. So much for her thoughts of Sandy. They had been idle dreams, formed in her imagination, and she was a sentimental fool to have entertained them. No wonder he hadn't phoned the previous evening. He had been dancing with Isobel, probably holding her as close as he had held Janice. That evening in Glasgow had meant nothing to him.

She was glad that she had promised to take the children to Blairochry that afternoon. She had to buy in some provisions, and the children, who wanted to spend their Saturday pennies made a pleasant distraction from her own troubled thoughts.

It was Janice's first stroll around the little town and, even in her mood, she liked what she saw of it. Blairochry sat on either side of the river Erdal, which was fairly broad at this point, spanned by a fine stone bridge. There was a pleasant green stretch along one bank, and a river-walk which was popular with visitors.

Janice completed her shopping and carried her purchases to the car. Then came the important business of the afternoon, at least in the children's eyes. Saturday pennies were not to be lightly spent, and a great deal of window shopping and comparison of values had to be gone through before any purchase was made. Eventually they were all satisfied that they had obtained the best possible value for their money.

The little town was busy, as was usual on a Saturday, when people from the surrounding districts came in to do their weekend shopping. Mary held Robbie tightly by the hand, which he kept struggling to release, in order to eat potato crisps from the bag in his other hand. Every few seconds there was a disagreement.

'Come on,' Janice said finally. 'Let's walk by the river for a little. There aren't any cars there, and you needn't hold Robbie's hand and he can finish his crisps.'

Everyone thought this a good idea, and they all enjoyed a brisk walk in the pale winter sunshine. When the crisps were eaten, they chased one another over the grass till all were breathless and rosy-cheeked.

As they returned to the car, Mary tapped Janice's arm.

'There's Mr Nicol,' she said.

Janice felt her heart jump as she looked to where Mary was pointing. There, indeed, was Sandy in his Land-Rover, but he hadn't spotted them. Hurriedly, as an encounter with Sandy was the last thing she wanted, Janice tried to shepherd the children out of sight. It was too late.

'Mr Nicol!' said Paul, in his clear boy's voice and Sandy, who was waiting to turn at an intersection, heard him. He leaned out of the car window, calling to them:

'Hang on, till I find somewhere to park.' He drove round the corner, out of sight.

'Come along children,' Janice said briskly. 'Back to the car. We must get off home.'

'But Mr Nicol—' Robbie began to protest.

'We haven't time just now. We'll see him another time. Hurry up now!'

Janice knew that her tone was sharp

and the children were giving her puzzled glances. Paul tried again.

'Mr Nicol is going to wonder where we've gone. And he's gone to all the bother of finding a parking space!'

'Don't argue, Paul. Mr Nicol will understand.' Janice tried to sound convincing, which was hard, as she knew she was in the wrong, but she couldn't face Sandy. She hustled the mutinous trio into the car and hurriedly started the engine. As she drove out of the car park and up the street, she caught sight of a puzzled Sandy standing on the pavement, looking around him.

'There he is! He's seen us!' cried Paul, just as Janice rounded the corner, out of view.

Well, thought Janice. I've certainly burned my boats now, and misery flooded over her. Why, oh why did this man spark off such violent reactions in her? He was sure to guess the cause of her behaviour, and know that she was jealous. She had no cause to feel so strongly about someone she had only just met, and who felt only friendship towards her. After this incident, she had probably destroyed even that friendship.

The children were quiet and Janice could sense their puzzlement. She had hardly set them a good example of manners. However, their good spirits returned slowly, and they started a game of "I spy".

They were nearing the turn-off to the hotel, when they rounded a bend in the road, and all stared in surprise. A man in an orange jacket was controlling the traffic, as half the road was blocked by a large lorry. Janice slowed to a crawl and looked to see what was going on. Scaffolding had been erected at the side of the road and several men were preparing to fix into position a huge board painted in glowing colours. As they approached the sign, for hotel sign it was, was raised up for them to see. It read:

Drive straight on for the first Euroscot Hotel. Under this, in smaller letters, Janice just had time to read *Continental Cuisine,* before being waved on. Some yards behind this monster, completely dwarfed by it, was the Kirkton House Hotel sign, pointing hopefully in another direction.

The children were talking excitedly, happily unconscious of the sign's implications.

'It's a super sign, isn't it?' was Paul's comment.

'The colours are lovely. Wish I could paint as nice as that.' Robbie was wistful.

They stopped at the side of the hotel, and as Janice unloaded the provisions, the children hurried in the side entrance. By the time Janice entered, Hugh had already heard the news.

'Is it really as eye-catching as all that?' he asked Janice quizzically.

She nodded.

'I'm afraid so.'

'Ah well,' said Hugh. 'I've already made my decision. I phoned Herr Traub this afternoon, and informed him of it. It may not be the right decision, but I stand by it.'

Janice stared at Hugh but his face was, as usual, devoid of any expression which could give her a clue to his thoughts. Hugh looked back at her for a moment, then turned and spoke to the children, who were animatedly describing the new hotel-sign to Annie Mackay.

'Hang up your anoraks,' he said, 'and wash your hands for tea. Miss Janice and I have something to discuss in my office.'

As Janice followed Hugh through, she realised how much his decision would affect her future. She couldn't imagine that the Swiss company would allow things to continue just as they were at Kirkton House. Suddenly she knew just how involved she had become with the Murray family, and with the future of the hotel. She hated the thought of being rootless and homeless once more.

In the office, Hugh kept her further in suspense.

'I had to weigh all the factors,' he told her, and proceeded to do so again for her benefit.

Janice felt herself gripping the edge of the table in an effort not to show her mounting impatience, as he listed all the pros and cons.

'To sum up,' he finally said, 'it was quick financial gain on one side, against being my own boss and keeping a way of life I enjoy. I've therefore decided,' he paused, and Janice held her breath, 'to go it alone, and spare no effort to make a success of the hotel.'

'Oh,' said Janice in relief, 'I am glad, Hugh. I'm sure you can build this place up again and make it as successful as it ever was. I'll do everything I can to help you.'

'Thank you,' he replied simply, and gave her one of his rare, warm smiles.

'What did Herr Traub say when you told him?' asked Janice.

'Well, he said the offer would remain open in case I should change my mind, which was very fair of him in the circumstances,' replied Hugh. 'Although I wish he wasn't quite so sure that I will.' He pulled some papers towards him, and his voice resumed its serious tone.

'We'll have to arrange to have some temporary staff over the Christmas season,' he said. 'Usually we can get several local girls who are at home from college. We'll need extra this year for the ski-annexe.'

'I've been thinking about the ski-annexe,' broke in Janice eagerly. 'What about sending a publicity letter to the ski-clubs in the cities? They're the kind of people who might like the idea of an inexpensive holiday over the New Year, and we could get block bookings from them.'

Hugh Murray nodded, making a note as he said, 'That's a good idea. I'll get letters off right away.'

When Janice returned to the kitchen to give the children their meal, she was feeling quite happy, the episode in Blairochry that afternoon, when she had reacted so childishly towards Sandy, was pushed to the back of her mind. There would be plenty to do to help her keep it there. Work, she told herself, is a marvellous anaesthetic. Soon she'd remember the whole affair without pain.

Next morning was Sunday. After breakfast, Janice made dozens of mince-pies, which she would deep-freeze till Christmas. The children, who seemed to have forgotten about her peculiar behaviour in Blairochry, drifted into the kitchen one by one. Paul brought his fort and soldiers and Mary brought a jig-saw, while Robbie was, as usual, making a picture.

'What are you drawing today?' asked Janice, as she cut out rounds of pastry.

'A pattern with lots of lovely colours,' Robbie told her.

'I think he's going to be an artist, like Daddy,' volunteered Paul, who was engrossed in waging a full-scale battle between opposing armies.

'Like your Daddy?' echoed Janice, in surprise.

'Oh, yes. Didn't you know?' asked Mary, looking up from her jig-saw.

'He's illustrated books, you know.' There was pride in Paul's tone.

'What kind of books?'

'Books of flowers, the kind that grow wild. And trees. Some animals, too. But flowers are his best thing.'

Janice's hands went on cutting out pastry rounds, while her mind registered astonishment. She didn't know any artists, but the very word conjured up pictures of eccentric dress and unusual behaviour. Certainly her idea of an artist was far removed from the reserved, self-possessed Hugh Murray. He certainly was a man with hidden depths.

Deftly, Janice shaped the mince-pies, and packed them for the deep-freeze. Soon she'd be busy making Christmas cakes and puddings. With a full-house and, she hoped, a busy ski-annexe, they would have to be well organised for Christmas.

After clearing up, it was time for Janice to tidy herself. She was taking the children to Sunday School that morning, and attending the service herself. She wasn't a regular church-goer, somehow the habit had never been formed in London, but her upbringing made her no stranger to the service.

Although Kirkton Church was small, it had the simple beauty of stone, wood and glass, plus many generations of loving care. Janice and the children were welcomed, and she recognised several people from the bonfire.

While Janice waited for the children outside the church, Isobel Dawson emerged with a very attractive woman. As her companion paused to speak to the minister, Isobel hurried over to Janice and introduced her to various members of the congregation.

'Have you met Mr and Mrs Anderson, from the post office?' she asked.

Janice had not, and was introduced to this pleasant couple, who were "incomers" to the Glen, having spent their younger days in Dundee.

The children had arrived at her side, and made their goodbyes as they climbed into the car.

'See you on Wednesday!' called Isobel, and Janice nodded and waved.

The beginning of the week was busy, as the soft furnishings arrived from Glasgow, and the finishing touches were added to the ski-annexe. When all was complete, Hugh and Janice toured the new addition to the hotel with some satisfaction. The colours blended well, and even on this dim November afternoon the rooms looked welcoming and cheerful.

'If only the customers come,' Hugh remarked, drily.

'If only the snow comes!' added Janice.

'Did you write to the ski-clubs?'

'Yes. And of course, I'd already circularised schools and colleges who might

94

come during term time. I've had quite a few responses from them. It all depends, as you remarked, on snow conditions. If we don't get the snow, this could be a great big white elephant.' Hugh sounded gloomy.

'What about the rest of the year?'

'Well, I hope to interest the education authorities in doing field studies from here. The Glens around are full of interest for the naturalist.' He paused and added, 'It's an interest of mine, actually.'

'Yes,' answered Janice, matching his tone. 'The children told me. You do illustrations, don't you?'

'Mostly textbooks.' He nodded, then he seemed to want to change the subject, away from himself. 'Do you think, if school-children come that they'll be content to stay here in the evenings?' His eyes indicated the deep window-seats, and points for a record player which had been provided in both dormitories.

'Oh, I should think so,' said Janice. 'Teenagers like a place of their own. I don't think they'd like mixing with the other guests downstairs in the lounge in the evenings.

'With their own showers and drying room, they'll only come over to the main building for meals, really, and the dining-room can cope easily.'

That evening, when she had finished clearing up after a few dinner-guests, Janice hurried to her room to change for her visit to Kirkton Schoolhouse. She put on a woollen dress in a deep blue shade, one of her favourites.

She was thinking about Isobel's mother. 'An unusual woman' had been Sandy's description. She couldn't help wondering what it must feel like to live so close to the house and estate which had once been your home?

She drove down to the school through the dark frosty night. There was a mistiness in the darkness, and Janice drove with extra care on the twisting road.

The schoolhouse stood some yards away from the school building, and a little gate opened on to a path which led to the front door. As she rang the bell, Janice felt rather apprehensive. Isobel, though always pleasant, was still largely a stranger to her. The prospect of an evening in her company and that of her 'unusual' mother was rather daunting. Then, there was Isobel's relationship with Sandy...Her thoughts were terminated by the opening of the door, and Isobel standing in a beam of light, smiling in welcome.

The house was fairly old, and Janice liked it at once. There was a cheerful, open fire crackling on the hearth in the sitting-room and Janice sank with an appreciative sigh into a comfortable, chintz-covered armchair.

Isobel sat down on the other side of the fire and smiled at Janice.

'Tired?' she asked.

'I believe I am,' said Janice, 'although I hadn't realised it till I sat down! We've been pretty busy this week, completing the ski-annexe.'

'Oh, yes,' said Isobel, 'where the stables used to be. How has it turned out?'

Janice described the accommodation and furnishings.

'It's been on the go for a long time,' remarked Isobel. 'I think it was Sheila's idea, Hugh's wife, you know. After the accident though, he just lost interest for a while.'

'Did you know Sheila?' asked Janice.

'Everyone here knew her. She was a friendly kind of person—quite different from Hugh. But they seemed to complement each other. He was shattered after the accident.' Isobel stared into the fire.

'I can imagine,' said Janice quietly. After a pause, she added, 'What do you think about Mary's behaviour these days? Do you think she's improving, or did that firework incident set her back?'

'It's difficult to say.' Isobel frowned. 'She still smothers Robbie. I really don't know how long it can go on, because he's such an independent little boy, and can do more and more for himself. How is she with you?'

'She doesn't feel much either way about me personally,' said Janice, slowly. 'As long as I don't interfere with Robbie, we get on quite well. She's sometimes quite friendly, but it's all on her terms.' Janice was quiet, thinking.

'She said something to me after the accident which I don't understand. It seemed terribly important to her. She kept saying that she'd promised to look after him. At the time, I thought she meant she'd promised me to look after Robbie at the bonfire, but then I remembered she'd done no such thing,' Janice sighed. 'I suppose it'll sort itself out eventually.'

'I certainly hope so,' agreed Isobel. 'She was such a happy little girl before her mother died.'

She glanced at her watch. 'Mother should be back soon. She's just gone to visit a neighbour. I'll put on the kettle when she comes in.'

They chatted for some time, and, naturally, the subject of the new hotel cropped up. Isobel thought that it was a very real threat to Kirkton House, and echoed Sandy's sentiments about people being more interested in a bright, modern new place.

'Still!' she added, perhaps noticing Janice's worried expression, 'I don't see why there shouldn't be room for both.'

At that moment, the door opened, and the attractive woman who had been with Isobel in church entered the room. Her dark hair was swept up and was held in a loose chignon.

'Oh, Mother,' said Isobel, 'This is Janice Taylor. Janice, this is my mother.'

'How are you, Janice?' said Mrs Dawson, her hand outstretched in greeting.

Janice, who had been vaguely expecting someone of her own mother's generation, felt her face register complete astonishment, as she stammered out a greeting. This woman couldn't be more than a youthful thirty-five, she was sure!

Mrs Dawson seemed to see and appreciate Janice's surprise, because she laughed gaily.

'It's quite true,' she said. 'I AM her mother. You see I was very young when I married.'

'She's always being taken for my sister,' put in Isobel. 'I only hope it's a family trait!'

They all laughed and Janice felt her confusion dissolve. Mrs Dawson, far from thinking her rude, obviously had enjoyed the surprise which Janice had shown. She must be well used to this reaction from people meeting her for the first time.

'I'll put the kettle on now,' said Isobel. 'You keep Janice company, Mother. I won't be a minute.' She disappeared to the kitchen.

In the soft lamp-light, the truth about Isobel's mother was hard to believe. Even if she had been married at seventeen, she must now be at least forty-five. Janice tried hard not to stare, and searched for some topic of conversation, but Mrs Dawson spoke first:

'I believe you are living in my former home. There will be many changes inside, I suppose, but from the outside it is quite unaltered in appearance.'

'It's a beautiful house,' said Janice impulsively. 'I'm glad it hasn't been spoiled.'

'It was built by my husband's grandfather, you know,' continued Mrs Dawson. 'He designed it himself.'

She paused, and looked straight at Janice.

'I suppose you've already heard the story of how it became a hotel?'

Janice nodded. 'Yes, Sandy Nicol

mentioned it. You must find it strange, living so near.'

Mrs Dawson looked at her in silence for a moment. The lovely face hardened, and there was an intensity in her voice when she spoke again.

'We shall not leave this Glen. Kirkton House is where my daughter was born. It was her birthright, taken from her by cruel circumstances. Some day it will be restored to her.'

Janice stared at her, shocked by the certainty in her voice. What could she mean by such a statement? As if conscious of Janice's thoughts, Mrs Dawson gave a short laugh and rose, walking slowly across the room.

'People don't think I'm serious. Even Isobel doesn't quite understand. But mark my words, it will happen as I say!'

At this moment, Isobel returned, wheeling a laden trolley. She glanced from one to another, as if sensing the tension in the air.

'Mother,' she said, smiling ruefully, 'have you been letting your Hebridean ancestors take over again?' She turned to Janice.

'Mother's grandmother had the Second Sight, and she can't forget it!'

Janice was glad to join in the laughter as conversation returned to normal.

'Are you from the Hebrides, Mrs Dawson?' Janice asked to keep the conversation light.

'I lived all my early life on Lewis, where my father worked a croft. I came to Perth at sixteen to live with a relative, and I met my husband there. He was much older than me, but we married the following year.

'Did you see Isobel's photo in the paper on Saturday?' Mrs Dawson asked suddenly.

Janice felt her face tense a little, but she managed to smile as she answered.

'I thought it was a lovely photo, Isobel. Your dress looked beautiful.'

'Show it to Janice,' suggested Mrs Dawson. 'You can't appreciate its colours in a photograph.'

Isobel rose with some show of reluctance and left the room. Mrs Dawson turned to Janice and lowered her voice.

'Don't Isobel and Sandy Nicol make a handsome couple?'

'Yes, they do indeed,' Janice managed to reply.

'He's such a nice boy and they get on so well together. Of course, they've known each other for years. Almost childhood sweethearts!'

Janice was finding this conversation very difficult, and she greeted Isobel's return with the dress with immense relief. But her relief was premature, because Isobel, having caught the last remark, asked indignantly. 'Who are childhood sweethearts?'

Her mother looked up, a little taken aback.

'Why, you and Sandy,' she replied, rather uncertainly.

'Oh, mother,' said Isobel helplessly. 'What rubbish.' She turned to Janice.

'We're far from being sweethearts. We've known each other for ages, that's all. Sandy has to make an appearance at a lot of functions around here, and I quite often go with him. We arranged that Friday night several weeks ago, when a farmer presented Sandy with two tickets.'

Janice was utterly confused. Thankfully, she seized on the topic of Isobel's dress, admiring it and discussing current fashion trends, until it was time for her to go.

As Isobel went to get her guest's coat, Mrs Dawson again turned confidentially to Janice.

'I do admire you, staying at Kirkton House, quite unchaperoned!'

Janice stared into the charming, smiling face. What could she reply to such a remark, and what did Mrs Dawson mean by it?

As Isobel helped her on with her coat, Janice was conscious of being warmly invited to call at any time. She thanked Isobel and her mother, and made her way to the car, her mind in a turmoil.

Driving home, she reviewed her evening, wondering if the strangeness had been in her own mind. Was Mrs Dawson the pleasant person she seemed to be most of the time? Were the remarks she made during Isobel's absence meant well, or was there something behind them, which was not so pleasant?

CHAPTER 6

As Janice entered the hotel, Hugh called to her from his office. When she went in, she found him looking worried.

'We've been beaten to it,' he began. 'I decided to phone around today about temporary staff. I tried the usual families, but found I was a day too late! The opposition was busy yesterday and they've got it all sewn up.'

'But surely,' Janice began indignantly, 'if the girls usually come to you, they might have known you'd want them again!'

'That was my first reaction,' admitted Hugh. 'I felt rather disappointed in them, until I was tactfully reminded that I left them all in the lurch last year, when I closed the hotel over Christmas and New Year. I can't blame them, and anyway the new hotel would be an attractive change for those young girls.'

Janice stood, deep in thought. 'We could advertise,' she said slowly, 'but that would bring people from further away, and we just can't accommodate living-in staff. Are there no other girls in the Glen?'

Hugh shook his head. Suddenly an idea came to Janice. 'Girls!' she cried. 'Why does it need to be girls? Aren't there any boys coming home for the holidays?'

Hugh looked at her, a smile slowly dawning.

'Waiters, rather than waitresses?' he mused. Then he nodded. 'It could be possible. I can think of several possible lads from the village. I'll attend to it in the morning.'

He went to lock up, and Janice went thankfully to bed.

During the days that followed, Janice's idea proved to be a good one, and by the weekend the staffing position had been satisfactorily resolved. Janice and Annie Mackay had not been idle either, and all the Christmas baking was complete. Janice was glad her days were so full that she had little time for daydreaming about Sandy.

One afternoon, when she was working in the kitchen, there was a knock on the outside door. She hurried along the passage and opened it, and to her surprise, found Sandy standing on the threshold.

'Hello there,' he said, his voice very light. 'Is Hugh around? My feet are so muddy I didn't want to go in the front way.'

Janice surveyed his large rubber boots.

'Why not slip your boots off here?' she suggested. 'You can come into the kitchen while I fetch him.'

'No thanks,' was the reply. 'I'd like him to come out to the Land-Rover. I've got something to show him.'

'Very well. I'll tell him.' Janice turned hurriedly. She had been wrong to think she wouldn't be hurt again. Sandy's cool tone and guarded expression were so different from his usual warmth towards her.

Janice delivered the message to Hugh and returned to work in the kitchen. A few minutes passed and Janice heard

Hugh calling her. She hurried out and found the two men studying a handsome black labrador dog, who stood between them, tail wagging.

'Do you like dogs, Janice?' said Hugh, as Janice approached them.

Janice looked at the dog. His eyes were bright and his coat was glossy. He looked alert, fit and intelligent.

'If you mean *that* dog,' she answered carefully, 'yes, I do like him.'

She offered him her hand to sniff, then patted his sleek head while he gazed up at her with velvet eyes.

Both men sighed with relief.

'The children have been wanting a dog for a while,' explained Hugh. 'I asked Sandy to keep an eye open for a suitable mature dog, because we couldn't take on a pup. It had to be used to sleeping in a kennel, as it couldn't have the run of the hotel. Also, it had to be reliable with children, and if possible trained to the gun.'

'Quite a tall order!' chipped-in Sandy. 'It was just luck that a family in Blairochry are moving to the city. The house that they're moving to isn't suitable for a big dog, and they asked me to find a good home. This should do you, eh, Jet?'

Hugh glanced at his watch.

'It's time I collected the children,' he said. 'I'm sure Janice will give you a cup of tea, Sandy. The kettle's usually on at this time!'

'Of course!' said Janice, brightly. For a moment it looked as though Sandy might refuse, but after a pause he accepted the invitation. Leaving Jet in the Land-Rover, he took off his muddy boots, and followed Janice into the kitchen.

It was Annie's day off and, as Janice busied herself, she was conscious of his eyes following her. He was very quiet. Janice was searching her mind frantically wondering what to say should the subject of their last encounter be raised. When finally he broke the silence.

'Do you know about dogs?'

'No, not really. Being brought up in a flat in Glasgow I never had one of my own.I used to long for one when I was about ten, and I never could understand why my parents wouldn't let me have it.'

She knew she was gabbling, but she couldn't help herself. Sandy answered quietly, explaining about feeding, grooming and exercise. Janice poured the tea and sat down at the other end of the table, wishing the children would come.

'I visited the schoolhouse on Wednesday,' she said at last. 'It's a charming house, isn't it? And Mrs Dawson is an amazing woman.'

Sandy looked at her. 'In what way?' he asked, unhelpfully.

'Well, it's hard to believe she's Isobel's mother. She looks more like a slightly older sister!'

'Oh, you mean her appearance,' said Sandy.

'Not only her appearance.' Janice suddenly found courage to be frank. 'She said some rather strange things, too.'

'I warned you, didn't I?' he said, looking almost like the Sandy she knew. 'Mrs Dawson is someone to be careful about. Careful what you say to her, and careful what you listen to. I often think...'

But what Sandy thought was lost in the excited arrival of the children, anxious to meet their new pet. As Janice watched Sandy introduce them to Jet, showing them how to pat him, explaining patiently how to treat a dog of this kind, she knew she wanted his friendship on any terms. Perhaps this was one of the things Sandy was warning her not to believe. She knew from his attitude that she had offended him deeply by her behaviour.

Just then, Hugh Murray came to Janice's side. Sandy looked over at them.

'Are you putting Jet into the old kennels?' he asked, 'I brought his own bed with me, to make him feel more at home.'

'I'll need a work squad to clean the kennels and make them comfortable for him,' said Hugh, smiling at his children.

There was no lack of volunteers. Soon the three were busy at work, sweeping and cleaning the kennel and run, then carrying Jet's bed to install it in his new home.

'It's a nice little house for Jet,' conceded Robbie, 'but I'd rather have him at home. He'd be much cosier in the kitchen!'

'He'd be too cosy!' Sandy told him. 'Jet's always been used to kennels. As long as he has a warm bed and there is no damp or draught, he'll be much healthier outside.'

'Anyway,' added Janice, 'you can't have a dog around a hotel kitchen, where food is being prepared and cooked. It's against the law.'

'Now you three can put on Jet's lead and take him for a short walk up the hill,' said their father. 'Don't be long, and don't let him off the lead.'

The three went off with Jet, taking turns to hold the lead.

'I can't thank you enough, Sandy,' said Hugh.

'That's all right,' said Sandy. 'I solved two families' problems by bringing him here!'

He made his way to the Land-Rover, waving goodbye. Hugh went into the hotel, but Janice stood, watching him go. He started the engine, then looked up and saw her still there.

'Janice,' he called softly, switching off the motor, as she went over to him. He seemed to be searching for words, and he gripped the steering wheel.

'I don't know why I'm telling you,' he began, 'but anyway, I'm going to be away for a bit. I'm going on a course about developments in the treatment of animal diseases—I won't bore you with details, but I'll be away for about ten days.'

'Where is it being held?' asked Janice.

'London. I'll stay with my sister and brother-in-law.' He stopped, seeming to have more to say, but being unable to put it into words. The happy voices of the children floated down from the hill as dusk began to fall.

Sandy bent forward with an abrupt movement, and switched on the engine.

'Well, goodbye, Janice.'

'Goodbye, Sandy. Enjoy yourself in London.'

'Thank you.' The Land-Rover moved a few yards, then stopped. He leaned out, speaking quickly, his voice rather husky so that Janice had difficulty catching what he said.

'About Saturday, I got the message. I won't bother you again.'

He was away, the wheels of the Land-Rover spinning a little on the gravel.

Janice turned blindly and went back into the hotel. Sandy had believed the only logical explanation of her strange behaviour. He thought that she had purposely rebuffed him. And she was powerless to do anything about it...

CHAPTER 7

In the days following Sandy's departure South, Janice found a strange kind of peace. It was as though she'd accepted that there was absolutely nothing to be done about the misunderstanding meanwhile, and with Sandy so far away, there was no possibility of a chance encounter. She could see a Land-Rover draw up at the hotel without reaction, and her visits to Blairochry were undisturbed by glimpses of fair-haired men wearing tweed jackets.

There was still little doing at Kirkton House Hotel. There were no resident guests, and few people for meals, except at weekends or the occasional shooting party. The latter presented a new problem. Lately, Mary had become terrified by the sound of guns, although all the shooting was well away from the hotel, high on the hill.

'Do you think it could have any connection with Robbie's accident on bonfire night?' Janice asked Hugh when she went to see him about it.

'I suppose it could,' Hugh answered thoughtfully. 'The sound is very similar to the noise made by a firework.'

Janice sighed. She wondered when the repercussions of that night—when, she felt, her lack of vigilance had contributed to the accident—would finally be over. Hugh heard the sigh and looked at her thoughtfully.

'How are you getting on with Mary now?' he asked.

'Oh, well enough, I suppose. She seems to have accepted me fairly well, but I still feel that I don't really know her.'

The arrival of the morning post put an end to their discussion. There was an envelope addressed to Janice, and Hugh handed it to her before taking the rest of the mail into his office.

It was a square, white envelope which felt rather stiff, and the name and address were in an unfamiliar hand. It had a local postmark and Janice carried it to the kitchen, trying to guess the contents. However, Annie Mackay engaged her in conversation and she laid it aside to open later. Then she became so caught up in her morning's work that the envelope was still unopened an hour later when Hugh sought her out, an identical envelope in his hand.

'Take a look at this,' he said, handing it to her with eyebrows raised.

The envelope contained a thick card with a gold rim. It was an invitation to a reception to mark the opening, the following week, of the new Euroscot Hotel. A well-known television personality was to attend the gathering too.

'I think,' Janice said as she returned the card to Hugh, 'that I've also been honoured!' She found her envelope and confirmed that it also contained an invitation.

'Well,' remarked Hugh. 'They're certainly doing things in style. We must both go, of course. It's from three to five o'clock. You can look after things here, can't you, Annie, with Etta to help? We'll be only a phone call away.'

'Och, I can do that all right, Mr

Murray,' said Annie.

Hugh began to walk out of the kitchen, then turned and said to Janice in a hesitant manner.

'Can you spare a minute? I've had some other news this morning.'

Janice followed him to the office.

'Sit down for a moment,' he invited, as he took his usual chair. He picked up an opened airmail letter, then studied it again for a few seconds, in silence.

'This is from my parents,' he began at last. 'My father has been working in the Bahamas for the past ten years. He's with the Civil Service. Now his job there is almost finished, and he's opted to retire.'

'Will your parents be coming to Scotland?' Janice asked.

'No. My father, having been used to warmth, feels that the South of England would probably be wiser for him. Then, there are my sisters.'

'Oh!' Janice was surprised at the discovery of all the relatives. Hugh had seemed such a loner that she hadn't expected him to have any family other than his children.

'My sisters are a lot younger than I am,' Hugh went on. 'They're twins too. They'll be about twenty now, I suppose.' He had the usual male vagueness about ages, Janice noted.

'To tell you the truth,' he continued in a tone which, for him, was very confiding, 'I'm afraid I don't really know them very well. I was a teenager when they were born, and didn't pay much attention to them. When they were about ten, my parents went abroad, and I've only seen them for short visits since. Still,' his tone became judicious, 'they seem to be pleasant enough girls.'

Janice couldn't help laughing at this and after a surprised moment Hugh joined in, looking sheepish.

'I know it must sound peculiar,' he admitted. 'We're not exactly a close family.'

Later, Janice wondered about this conversation. Hugh was not usually so forthcoming about personal matters, and his news surely had no bearing on affairs at the hotel. Perhaps, a year after Sheila's death, he was just learning to communicate with people again. He had a great deal in common with his little daughter, Janice reflected.

That Saturday, there was to be a shoot, over the hill above the hotel. Janice knew that this would worry Mary, and she planned to keep her busy indoors, doing various chores. Although there was never any shooting near the hotel, the sound echoed in the hills, and Mary obviously found it frightening. It was therefore a very pale little girl who sat at the table in the hotel kitchen, toying with her lunch.

Paul and Robbie were discussing Jet, their new labrador.

'Mr Nicol told us not to let him off the lead for at least two weeks,' Paul was telling Robbie, who looked sulky. 'He has to learn that this is where he belongs now. If we let him off too soon he might run back to his old home again.'

'Jet wouldn't do that. He likes it here!' Robbie protested. 'And he likes us—I know he does. He wouldn't want to run away.'

'You'd better do as Mr Nicol said,'

Janice advised. 'He knows best. Anyway, you can't take Jet on the hill today when the shoot's on. Just take him as far as the bottom dyke. Are you going with the boys, Mary, or will you help me clear up?'

'I think I'll just stay and help you,' said Mary, relieved.

Paul and Robbie went out with Jet's lead, and Janice chatted to Mary, trying to bring her out of herself, but it was even more difficult than usual. They had just finished taking the clean plates of out of the dish-washer when Paul came in.

'Where's Robbie?' asked Mary sharply.

'Outside with Jet, of course. I just came in for...'

'You shouldn't have left him by himself!'

She ran towards the door and, as she went, shots echoed from half-a-mile away. Mary's hands covered her ears and she swung round to face Janice.

'They're shooting,' she screamed, 'and Robbie's out there!'

She was gone, before Janice could

122

utter the words of reason which would assure her that there couldn't be the slightest danger. There was nothing to do but follow her.

As Janice came out of the hotel she could see Robbie and Jet at the bottom dyke, nowhere near the guns. Mary was making towards them as quickly as she could. The shooting party was high on the hill, moving in a direction away from the hotel. Robbie was bent over Jet and, as Janice hurried towards them, he straightened up, Jet's unclipped lead in his hand.

Jet, now free and hearing the familiar sound of guns, pricked up his ears and was off, over the dyke, in the direction of the shooting party.

'Jet, come here!' commanded Robbie, unaware that Janice was behind him. He climbed over the dyke in pursuit.

'Robbie!' Mary screamed. 'Come back! You'll get hurt!'

As if to give emphasis to what she said, another burst of fire echoed round the hill.

Meanwhile Jet, torn between his training as a gun dog and his obedience to his new little master, stopped about twenty yards from the dyke, his tail wagging tentatively. Mary, too, stopped in her tracks, her dreadful fear of the sound, almost beating the desire to save Robbie from the danger she imagined.

Janice, who had almost reached Mary, opened her mouth to call assuringly to her when Mary suddenly ran forward again, her voice ringing out strongly, as her love for Robbie overcame her fear of guns and gunfire.

'Robbie, come back to the dyke. I'll fetch Jet.'

Resolutely she climbed over the dyke and with sudden wisdom, Janice let her go. The danger was all in Mary's mind, but that didn't make the fear any easier to overcome. She was as much a heroine as she would have been if the guns had been nearby.

As Mary approached Jet, he trotted over to her, and she led him by the collar back to the dyke where Janice and Robbie stood. She was pale and trembling a little, but, as the guns rang out again, she didn't flinch. With a business-like air she took the lead from an unresisting Robbie and clipped it to Jet's collar once more.

As they returned to the hotel, Janice was reminded of the return from the bonfire on that eventful evening, when Mary had been distraught and inconsolable; now that she had coped with the situation, she was composed, and her eyes were shining.

Back at the hotel, Hugh had to hear the whole story of Mary's bravery. Robbie, very chastened, and fighting back tears, was severely scolded for his disobedience.

'But why did you do it?' Hugh asked, puzzled.

'I just didn't want Jet to go back to his other house. I knew he liked it here, but I just wanted to be sure. And he didn't run back, did he? So he must like us best!' Robbie smiled at the thought.

That night, when Janice looked in to the children's bedroom she found Mary, as usual, not yet asleep. As she went over to the bed, Mary looked up at her, and Janice noticed thankfully that she was relaxed and sleepy.

'Not asleep yet?' Janice asked softly.

'No. I'm just thinking,' Mary whispered shyly. 'I'm thinking that I kept my promise after all.'

"The promise", again this word had cropped up. Obviously it was very important to Mary.

'What was your promise, Mary?' Janice asked tentatively, hoping that this direct question wouldn't cause Mary to retreat into her shell once again.

'I promised to look after Robbie. I told you.' Mary sounded puzzled that Janice should have to ask again.

'Oh yes, I remember. But who did you promise?'

'My mummy. It was on the day when she never came home. She was going in the car and we were playing at the back, and she said look after Robbie for her, and I promised. Then she went away...' Mary's voice shook a little, but she took a deep breath and continued:

'So I had to keep my promise, you see. And I did, today.'

'Yes, Mary, you did.' Janice's voice was unsteady. 'Mummy would have been proud of you. But she didn't mean that you have to look after Robbie all the time. She'd want you to play and have fun with your own friends.'

'Miss Janice is right,' said a voice, and Hugh Murray appeared beside them. 'It's my job to look after Robbie and Paul and you, too, Mary. And now I have Miss Janice to help me. You've kept your promise, Mary.'

He talked on gently to his little daughter, and Janice slipped out of the room. She felt quite shaken when she thought of the tremendous burden the little girl had carried for almost a year. Perhaps now she'd be able to relax a little, and allow others to share that load.

When Janice came down from the bedroom, the phone was ringing. It was Isobel, with an invitation for Janice to a social evening, given by the local Women's Rural Institute, at which a one-act play would be presented by the drama group.

'I know it can't compare with the West End productions you'll be used to seeing,' Isobel said, laughing. 'But honestly, I think you'll enjoy the evening.'

'I'm sure I shall,' Janice assured her. 'I'll look forward to it. It was kind of you to think of asking me.'

As Janice replaced the phone, she felt very cheered. Isobel was certainly going out of her way to be friendly and to make sure that Janice became part of the Glen community. She turned, to find Hugh walking towards her. He looked very happy and gave her a warm smile.

'I think you've done it,' he told Janice. 'You've made the breakthrough and got Mary to talk her worry out. I don't know how you managed it, but I'm more than grateful.'

'I don't think it was anything I did, particularly,' Janice objected. 'It was just the excitement of what happened this afternoon that brought things to a head. Mary's confidence got a tremendous boost and she felt able to talk about things at last. I just happened to be there at the right time.'

'Well, however it happened, it has made a great change in her. We had a real talk just now. I think that tonight I really got close to her.'

In the days that followed, there was indeed a dramatic change in Mary. It was as if she had decided that her duty had been well done, and that she had no further responsibility at all for Robbie. He, naturally, was confused by the situation. He had grown used to her fussing and, although he had protested when it interfered with his freedom, he had assumed that she'd always be at his beck and call. To find that he no longer had a willing slave made him a very puzzled little boy for a week or so.

The following week, Isobel remarked on the change in the children, as she and Janice sat in Kirkton Village Hall, before the start of the play.

When the lights in the hall were put out, the audience settled down to give all its attention to the play. It was a simple plot, and the pawky Scots humour of the script was well put over by the all-woman cast. One amazing factor was the performance given by Isobel's mother. In the leading part, she was absolutely convincing, and when, towards the end of the play, she sang a charming song, the audience was spell-bound.

The curtain closed, and as the enthusiastic applause rang out Janice turned to her companion.

'Your mother is marvellous,' she said sincerely. 'She could be a professional.'

Isobel, a little pink with natural pride, nodded in agreement.

'She really comes alive on the stage,' she said, and seemed to want to say more, but a great bustling broke out in the hall as chairs were re-arranged for the tea to follow.

There was quite a crowd, made up from husbands and friends of the cast, and also three visiting institutes. Kirkton W.R.I., had quite a reputation for drama, having won the area cup several times. The play presented that evening was to be their entry for the competition in the spring, and everyone present felt that it would be another success.

During tea, the talk soon turned to the opening, the following afternoon, of the new hotel. It appeared that almost everyone in the Glen would be present.

'I can't manage up for the opening

ceremony,' Isobel remarked disappointedly. 'School doesn't finish till three-thirty, but I should manage up about four o'clock.'

'The manager seems to be a nice lad,' a farmer's wife remarked. 'He came up to the farm asking about milk and eggs. What are you folk at Kirkton House Hotel thinking about all this?'

All eyes turned on Janice, who answered as confidently as she could, 'Oh, I don't think it'll affect us very much. It's a completely different type of place.'

'Yes,' said a sweet voice from behind Janice's shoulder, 'you and Hugh are quite the family concern, aren't you?'

Janice didn't need to turn to see who had spoken. She felt herself flush a little at the embarrassed titter which ran through some of the group, but she answered Mrs Dawson coolly and levelly.

'Well, yes. It's the family atmosphere that Mr Murray is aiming for. We obviously can't compete with the cosmopolitan image projected by the new place. But lots of people like the country house type of hotel, especially set in a Glen like this one. I hope there's room for both.'

There was a murmur of agreement from the group and Janice seized this opportunity to take her empty cup to a side table. She was amazed by her own calm reaction to what she could only believe was deliberate provocation by Mrs Dawson. She couldn't think why Mrs Dawson would want to rile her, but it was happening too often to be accidental.

Janice managed to circulate a little, chatting to those she had already met, and being introduced to new faces. She liked the people of this Glen. No one was gushing, but she was conscious of a quiet friendliness from most of them.

She found Isobel at her side once more, looking far from happy. Janice smiled at her.

'I've thoroughly enjoyed this evening, Isobel,' she assured her. 'Thank you very much.'

'Oh, I'm glad,' Isobel answered, then added with a rush, 'Please don't mind my mother. I sometimes don't know

what to make of the things she says.'
Her face was strained. 'She worries me,
Janice.'

Then, as if afraid of having said too
much, she stopped. 'I'm probably
making a storm in a teacup,' she said,
with forced cheerfulness. 'Well, see you
tomorrow at the reception.'

As Janice made her way back to the
hotel, she felt sympathy for Isobel. She
was worried about her mother's strange
behaviour, but obviously felt it would be
disloyal to discuss her with Janice. What
a strange woman Mrs Dawson was, with
her smiling face and her poisonous
tongue!

The following afternoon was the
opening of the new hotel. Hugh had
arranged for the children to be given a
lift home from school by a neighbour
and Annie and Etta would look after
them. Janice had dressed in her
favourite blue dress, and Hugh looked
very handsome in a cord jacket. It was
a cold, cheerless day with a heavy sky,
and shortly after three o'clock they
drove up the Glen.

To arrive at the new hotel was like

entering another world. As they drew up outside, the building glowed with warm light. They sat for a moment in the car, and Janice felt a little apprehensive and suspected that Hugh felt the same.

'Well,' he said, after a pause, 'let's face the opposition with our heads held high!'

As they entered, warm air caressed their chilled faces and they were aware of a great sense of space, while subdued background music combined with talk and laughter to give a festive air. Janice and Hugh were announced and then received by Herr Traub, who introduced them to his very smart wife, and then to the manager of the new hotel, Mark Proctor. He came from Yorkshire, and his charming manner combined with an attractive appearance made an excellent first impression. He'd certainly be an asset to any hotel, Janice thought.

They had just arrived in time. As they moved to join the company, Herr Traub held up his hand for silence. The television personality, who until now had been staying in the background, was ushered forward.

134

He somehow looked much smaller and less boyish than when seen on telivision, Janice thought.

Conversation ceased as heads turned to watch the ceremony. In his practised English, Herr Traub welcomed everyone, and spoke briefly about his hopes and plans for the first Euroscot Hotel. He then introduced Frank Dale, who spoke very wittily of some of the hotels in which he had stayed during his career in broadcasting.

After he drew the cork of a magnum of champagne to declare the hotel a going concern, he was presented with a gift and Frau Traub with a bouquet. Then the guests were invited to enjoy the buffet and to join in tours of the hotel.

Hugh and Janice helped themselves to the delicious buffet, which was attractively laid out. As they sat in luxurious leather chairs, Hugh broke in on Janice's thoughts, and asked her what she thought of the new hotel.

'So far, I'm most impressed. There's nothing cold or impersonal about this part of the hotel at least, and the staff seems very well trained.

'Will these be permanent staff?'

'I should think so. They'll have a skeleton live-in staff I should think, and the local girls will just help out at busy periods. Shall I get you something else to eat?'

'Mm—another of those, I think,' Janice said, pointing to the remaining smoked salmon roll on her plate. 'They're delicious.'

As Hugh went over to the buffet, Janice was joined by several local people, among them Isobel's mother. Her heart sank a little. She wanted to enjoy this afternoon without receiving a verbal thrashing from Mrs Dawson. She decided to get her word in first and opened the conversation by congratulating Mrs Dawson on her performance the previous evening.

Several others present joined in the praise, which was overheard by Herr Traub, who was circulating among the guests with Frank Dale in tow. Herr Traub was obviously in good spirits, being congratulated on all sides about the hotel.

'You are a fine singer?' he cried. 'Will

you not then honour us with a song? This is our first Scottish hotel. Why not have the traditional Scottish ceilidh to celebrate our opening?'

Everyone seemed to think that this was a splendid idea, although Janice considered that she'd never seen a less traditional setting for a ceilidh.

The piped music was stopped and Mrs Dawson was led to the wide steps which led to the dining area. Hugh had returned with Janice's smoked salmon which she hastily consumed before Mrs Dawson started.

Mrs Dawson stood on the step, not only looking calm and dignified, but very beautiful, and Janice was reminded of Isobel's remark that her mother 'came alive' on stage. As her voice, clear and sweet sang the 'Highland Fairy Lullaby,' Janice realised what a beautiful and talented woman she was. Frank Dale, who was standing beside Janice, obviously felt the same, and as Mrs Dawson left the steps to enthusiastic applause, he remarked to Janice, 'What a marvellous woman! Is she professional?'

'I don't think so,' Janice said. At that moment, Isobel arrived and Janice continued, 'But here's her daughter. She can tell you.'

She introduced Isobel and left them together discussing Isobel's mother. She and Hugh decided to tour the hotel, having a strong professional interest in it.

'Mr Murray,' Herr Traub said. 'Allow me to escort you round. And you, too, of course, Miss Taylor.'

The next half-hour was spent touring the whole place, kitchen included. It looked very well-planned, and easy to run, and the bedrooms were attractive and comfortable. Janice could see that Hugh was very impressed by the whole set-up. Sensing that Herr Traub would welcome a word with Hugh in private, Janice excused herself, and slipped away to rejoin the company.

As she came down the open stairs, two couples caught her eye. Mrs Dawson and the TV personality were deep in conversation on one settee, and Isobel was talking animatedly to Mark Proctor, the hotel manager, on another.

138

It was the second couple who held Janice's attention. Never had she seen Isobel look so animated, while Mark Proctor listened to her with smiling attention, which seemed for the moment to exclude all his responsibilities. Janice who had been about to join Isobel, changed her mind and started to cross to the other side, but Isobel caught her eye.

'Janice,' she called at once. 'Come and join us.'

As if brought back to reality with a start, Mark Proctor stood up and looked around him.

'I had better get back on duty!' he said ruefully. He turned back to Isobel. 'I'll see you soon,' he added significantly, and Isobel nodded happily.

As Janice sat down beside her, Isobel gave a little sigh.

'Isn't he nice?' she asked, frankly.

'Yes, he is. Is this his first hotel?'

'Well, the first he's been in charge of. He's been assistant manager in various hotels belonging to the same group, including one in Zurich and another in London.'

Just then, Hugh reappeared with

Herr Traub, who reclaimed Frank Dale from Mrs Dawson, who patted the seat beside her to indicate that Hugh should join her. With some reluctance, Janice thought, Hugh did.

'Our celebrity seemed most impressed by your mother,' Janice remarked to Isobel.

'Yes. He has a friend who's a producer with the B.B.C., who he thinks would like to hear her. I don't know how much influence he has, but Mother's quite thrilled.'

'I should think so! Perhaps this is the start of a fabulous career for her. How would you like to have a Television Celebrity for a mother?'

They both laughed. Suddenly Janice caught sight of Mrs Dawson and Hugh, who had been obscured by a group of people. She was talking intensely to him, and he looked startled and wary. He caught sight of Janice, and for a moment stared at her with questioning intensity, before looking away with a sudden movement. Janice knew, with a sick feeling in the pit of her stomach, that she was the subject of Mrs Dawson's conversation. Whatever she was saying had brought that old wariness back into Hugh's eyes, just when their relationship seemed to be taking on a friendly openness.

Hearing Isobel speak, Janice brought her attention back with an effort.

'I got a postcard from Sandy,' she was saying. 'He seems to be hating London, but enjoying seeing his sister and family again.'

'I don't think he's the London type of person,' Janice observed. Isobel gave her a quick, searching glance.

'You do like him, don't you?' she asked.

'Yes, of course I do.' Janice tried to keep her voice light. 'I think most people like Sandy.'

'Oh, I see,' said Isobel slowly.

Just then, Hugh approached them.

'I think we had better get down the road,' he said. 'It's after five o'clock.'

Having made their goodbyes, Hugh and Janice went out to the car. On the road down, Hugh was very quiet and when he did speak, the old formality was back in his manner. Janice was convinced she was right about Mrs Dawson's conversation and felt like cursing her for her mischief-making.

'Well, what are your final conclusions about the hotel?' she asked Hugh, in an effort to promote some communication with him.

'I'm very impressed. There's nothing cheap and shoddy about it. Herr Traub and I had a talk, and he has sound ideas on running hotels, shared I should think by his new manager. He is still interested in Kirkton House, by the way.'

'Are you having second thoughts?'

Hugh paused for quite a while before replying.

'I may be foolish, but I won't give in. I must make a success of Kirkton House Hotel. Then we shall see.'

'Can we make a success of it?'

They were drawing into the hotel car-park as his answer came.

'Given a good ski-ing season, we can.'

As if on cue, as they climbed out of the car, large feathery flakes began to fall, faster and faster, from the dark, winter sky.

CHAPTER 8

When Janice woke the next morning, she looked out on to a transformed world. During the night the snow had stopped falling, and frost had added a touch of brilliance to the whiteness. Janice, who had for so long been a city-dweller, was entranced by the purity of the scene; only the criss-crossing of animal tracks on the path below broke the surface of sparkling white.

The coming of snow had raised everyone's spirits. The two local women who cleaned every morning attacked their work with greater gusto than ever, Janice noticed. It had been dreary for them, following a cleaning routine in unused accommodation. In the kitchen, too, spirits were high as Janice told Mrs Mackay and Etta all about the Euroscot Hotel's grand opening.

Etta was being trained to cook during

this slack time and was showing some flair, and when the busy season started, she'd be able to relieve Annie Mackay.

When Hugh returned from running the children to school, he sounded a warning note.

'Don't expect skiers on the strength of one early snow-fall,' he told Janice. 'It takes a great deal more than an overnight fall to give good ski-ing conditions.'

Janice looked at him in dismay. She had been mentally preparing for a mass influx of skiers at the week-end, a quick thaw now would be too cruel.

'However,' Hugh added, 'the weather forecast sounds promising.'

By Friday, although the show had gone from Kirkton, there had been several heavy falls on the slopes. Two of the main runs were ski-able, while the nursery slopes were well-covered.

The phone started ringing on Friday morning and several rooms were booked, while the ski-annexe was reserved by a Glasgow Ski-Club. Only six guests would arrive for dinner on Friday evening, the rest having booked from Saturday.

This suited Janice perfectly, as she had the four schoolboys to train, and Friday evening would break them into the routine of waiting at table.

The four boys, all in their final year at Blairochry High School, arrived at the hotel after school on Friday. They looked very smart when they donned their white cotton jackets, with high collars and blue epaulettes, although they were all rather nervous.

Despite their fears of spilling soup over the guests, Friday's dinner went off without event, the four taking turns at serving the three tables.

When Janice told Hugh how well the evening had gone he seemed to be only half-listening. Since the reception at the new hotel, he had seemed ill-at-ease with her. Sometimes, Janice would look up from some task to find his eyes upon her, searching. He would look quickly away, leaving her with a most uncomfortable feeling. She was almost sure that his change of manner stemmed from something Mrs Dawson had said, but, having no proof, she didn't feel able to talk to him about it.

Now he was looking past her, frowning a little.

'Janice,' he said suddenly, then paused.

'Yes, Hugh?'

'Isobel's mother, Mrs Dawson. She's a peculiar woman, don't you find?'

'I certainly agree,' Janice replied coolly. 'She says the most outrageous things. I think it's best to take everything she says with a very large pinch of salt.'

'Do you?' Hugh's voice was eager. 'I think you may be right. She certainly said some peculiar things to me.'

He seemed about to continue, and Janice held her breath. Perhaps now they could clear the air and things would be as before. But her hopes were dashed. Just as he seemed on the point of confiding more, the new uneasiness came back to his eyes, and he turned abruptly away.

'I must lock up,' he said, without expression.

As Janice lay in bed, seeking sleep, her thoughts were disturbing. Had Mrs Dawson seriously harmed her relationship with Hugh? And what about Sandy? She tossed miserably. She had

146

only herself to blame for the ending of that friendship. It seemed that she had a genius for spoiled relationships, she thought, when she remembered Bryan, because even there she had reason to reproach herself. She was overcome by a wave of loneliness and self-doubt, before she finally fell into an uneasy dream-filled sleep.

The alarm clock shrilled through her dreams, and she rose wearily.

At breakfast, the children were full of plans for sledging on the hill. Their enthusiasm and happy chatter soon dispelled Janice's depression and as the busy day went on she had no time for gloomy thoughts.

It was marvellous to see the ski-annexe glow with light and hear the happy voices of skiers arriving from the slopes. The other residents were also skiers, and everyone mixed together in the comradeship of the sport.

The young waiters were happy to find themselves serving such a relaxed and friendly company and their confidence and skill grew.

By Sunday night the pressure was off again. There would be a quieter time until the following Friday, when the Glasgow Club was returning. This pattern of hectic weekends and quiet spells midweek repeated itself as they entered December and thoughts turned to Christmas preparations.

The year before, Christmas had been a sad time for the Murray family, coming as it did so soon after Sheila's tragic death. This year, Janice resolved, she'd make it a happy time for the children. Hugh and she planned to go to Dundee one afternoon to complete the Christmas shopping, an outing which seemed less attractive in view of the awkwardness which had grown between them.

One Thursday afternoon when Janice was checking the annexe to see that it was ready for its next occupants, Hugh called her.

'There's a man at reception asking for you,' he said.

Janice's thoughts flew unbidden to Sandy, before sense told her that he'd hardly enquire at reception. She was utterly unprepared for the surprise which awaited her.

'Bryan!' she gasped, and he turned, quickly and clasped her hands in his. His eyes looked searchingly into hers before he smiled.

'Janice! You do look well.'

'But how—where—who told you I was here?'

He laughed at her confusion.

'It's a long story. Can you get away for a while?'

'I think so. You wait in the lounge while I check with Hugh.'

She hurried off, full of pleasure and excitement at seeing Bryan once more. There was so much to ask, to explain, to hear about London and the people she knew there.

Hugh agreed at once that she should go.

'You haven't been taking enough time off,' he told her. 'It'll do you good to get away for a bit.'

If he was at all curious about Bryan, he certainly didn't show it. Janice dressed quickly and joined Bryan in the lounge. They went out to his car.

'Do you mind if we don't go far?'

Bryan asked when they were in his car. 'I left London before six this morning, and I must drive back tomorrow. I'm booked in at this new hotel up the road. What about going up there and having some afternoon tea, then just sit on till dinner? Could you bear to be as lazy as that? It would give us a chance to have a really long talk.'

'That would suit me perfectly,' Janice replied. 'I haven't got over my surprise at seeing you here yet. There are so many questions I want to ask.'

'Perhaps it would be best if I started from the beginning and told you the whole story,' Bryan suggested. 'But we'll wait till we're settled down with a nice cup of tea. You tell me how you come to be working here, at the back of beyond. Do you really like it?'

'Yes,' Janice said slowly as they drove up the Glen.

'Since the ski-ing season started, the world has come to us! There's plenty of company and lots to do.'

As they entered the new hotel they were greeted by Mark Proctor. Janice again thought what a pleasant person he was, secretly wondering if she was correct in thinking that there was a great attraction between him and Isobel Dawson.

As she and Bryan settled down to their afternoon tea, she was eager to hear his story.

'First,' he began, 'let me tell you about your letter. I finally got it last Friday! It must have arrived while I was on a marketing course. I lent the flat to a couple of pals for a week. They must have propped it up on the kitchen cabinet, and it got knocked off. Anyhow, I eventually found it down the back of the cabinet when I was fishing out a knife I'd dropped. I also found an income tax form the tax people kept asking me to return, and I kept telling them they'd never sent it.'

His tone changed, and he added quietly:

'I was sorry to read in your letter that your mother had died. I know how much she meant to you.' He paused, before continuing ruefully, 'Your opinion of me must have gone down a lot when I didn't write back.'

Janice answered frankly:

'I did feel a bit let down. But I thought you'd just got tired of writing letters which I didn't answer very regularly. I was to blame, too, though. Life just seemed so unreal, somehow, during those months in Glasgow.'

Bryan nodded sympathetically before continuing his story.

'When I found your letter, I just felt I had to see you and clear things up. I had the two days off and I phoned the Glasgow flat to find out if you could see me. I got a Mrs Thorpe, who explained she rented the flat and gave me your address and—well, here I am!'

He smiled at her. It began to dawn on Janice that Bryan had made a tremendous effort to put things right between them. The drive from London to Perthshire and back, just to see her, must mean that she was very important to him. The thought made her feel a little shy of him, and she looked down at her cup, confused.

'Tell me about London,' she said at last. 'How is the restaurant faring without me? Is your department still breaking records?'

They chatted like this for some time. Then Bryan asked, apologetically, 'Would you mind if I left you for half an hour? I'd like to shower and change before dinner. It would freshen me up and make me much better company. I'm in danger of falling asleep over the soup!'

Janice settled down to wait with an assortment of glossy magazines. She was rather pleased at the opportunity to see the new hotel function on a normal day.

She was so pleased at the chance to try and sort out her own emotions. Since Bryan had taken her by surprise, she hadn't had a moment to think clearly. Her main feeling was one of confusion. She was very happy to see Bryan again. He was so unchanged that all her former feelings towards him had come flooding back, and his obvious concern for her made her feel warm and cherished.

But what about Sandy? For weeks now, she'd carried a dull ache around with her; an ache which changed to pain if she let herself think about their broken friendship. During these weeks, she had thought only briefly of Bryan, and even then she'd regarded him as being part of her past.

Her chaotic thoughts were interrupted as Mark Proctor joined her for a few moments. They chatted for a short while and then, ever so casually, Mark introduced Isobel's name to the conversation. It seemed that he had been to the schoolhouse several times for supper, and when he spoke of Isobel he made no attempt to conceal his admiration for her.

'You should go in and see her sometime soon,' he added seriously. 'She thinks a lot of you, and I think she's worried just now.'

'Is it to do with her mother?'

'Yes.' He seemed relieved that he needn't explain. 'I think she'd like to talk to you about it.'

Just then, a refreshed Bryan joined them and Janice introduced the two men. As Mark left them to return to his duties he spoke to Janice.

'Shall I tell Isobel to expect you some evening?'

'Yes, I'll pop in soon,' Janice promised.

The dinner was most enjoyable; more

elaborate than Kirkton House could offer. Bryan was easy company and they had always got on well together, being interested in the same things. The atmosphere was light and friendly until the coffee arrived. Then a silence fell, to be broken by Bryan.

He leaned across the table, taking Janice's hand in his.

'Did I come in time?' he asked.

Janice looked at him. She wanted desperately to be truthful, to be able to tell him how she felt, but how could she explain her confusion, which made it impossible for her to give him an answer?

'Is there someone else for you now?' Bryan's voice was gentle.

There was a despairing note in Janice's voice as she answered at last.

'I just don't know! You see, when you didn't answer my letter, I thought it was because everything was over. And I came here and built a new life for myself. London and the times we shared seem so long ago.'

'But there's no-one else?' His voice was eager.

Janice looked down at their clasped

hands.

'I don't know.' Her voice was low. 'I did begin to think about someone...'

She broke off, and then added with a rush:

'I'm sorry, but I'm all confused. This is all so unexpected I'm afraid I just can't think straight at the moment.'

She looked at him, seeking understanding, and she saw it in his eyes.

'Don't worry, Janice,' he said. 'I know there's a chance for me. That's all that matters at the moment. This other chap has a fight on his hands!'

Janice smiled back at him. This was the Bryan she remembered, confident and determined.

'Now,' Bryan said, 'I'm taking you home. I've a long drive tomorrow, and I must have an early night, however unromantic that may be.'

As he released her hand to sign the bill, Janice sensed someone's eyes on her. She looked up to see Sandy. He was with some other men, and was looking intently at her. She looked back at him, her heart thumping. He smiled slightly, and nodded to her.

When Bryan held her chair, she rose automatically and allowed herself to be led out of the hotel. Her emotions had been so violently aroused during the past few hours that she could take no more. She felt quite numb.

Driving down the road, Bryan was in good spirits, making plans for meeting again.

'I'll come up in January,' he told her. 'I've some holidays still to come after sales week. But I'll phone you soon.'

He glanced at her in the dim light.

'Are you all right? You're very quiet.'

'I'm all right. Life has been rather fraught today, that's all.'

'I know and it was all my fault, popping in from the past like that.'

When they reached Kirkton House, he switched off the engine and headlights and took her in his arms. It was comforting to be held close and kissed by him.

'I've missed you,' he told her. 'I'll miss you even more now. But I'll phone you, and I'll see you in January.'

They kissed again before he saw her to the door. Then he was off into the night.

Janice stood at the hotel door for a while, enjoying the crisp air and watching the car lights appear and disappear as the car followed the tortuous road to the Glen.

She went quickly to bed, early as it was. She expected to toss and turn for hours, but almost at once she fell deeply asleep. In the morning she was glad to wake up to a busy weekend when she could shelve her personal problems for a while.

The following Tuesday evening, Janice decided to visit Isobel. She was pleased to find her friend alone so that they'd have a chance to talk without Mrs Dawson's presence. Isobel was delighted to see her.

'Do tell me about your mysterious stranger!' she began, almost as soon as Janice was in the door. 'You are a dark horse!

'And he came all the way from London, just to spend a few hours with you? He must be keen!' Isobel exclaimed, after Janice had explained what happened, then she added thoughtfully, 'Well, I must admit I'm a bit surprised. I had thought that you and Sandy

—but this puts a different complexion on things.'

'We're not engaged or anything,' Janice assured her. 'It was so unexpected that I haven't quite got things sorted out yet. No, I'm not being coy. I'm just not sure about anything at the moment. Anyhow, what about you? I gather that Mark has been a regular caller.'

Isobel blushed a little.

'There's nothing to tell, but we do seem to get on very well. It's early days, though.'

Janice nodded understandingly. She didn't probe.

'And how's your mother, Isobel? Any news from the TV people?'

Isobel's expression clouded.

'No, I'm afraid not,' she said sadly. 'Janice, I'm rather worried about Mother. She's even more cutting with her remarks than usual, these days.

'It's quite embarrassing at times.'

Isobel rose from her chair and crossed restlessly to a writing desk, where her fingers played nervously with the key as she continued:

'I think she felt that life was passing

her by, until this television thing cropped up, but the weeks are passing and she's heard nothing...'

Isobel turned to face Janice.

'I'm sorry to sound so miserable, but you see, she seems to resent you most of all.'

Janice looked up, surprised, but just as Isobel was about to explain herself, the doorbell rang.

'This could be Mark!' Isobel jumped up.

'He said he might manage in for a short time.'

She hurried out and it was several minutes before she re-appeared with Mark, who had his arm around her. They both looked very happy. After a while, Isobel rushed through to make coffee and left Mark and Janice chatting to each other. Suddenly the door opened and Mrs Dawson entered the room.

'Why, Mark!' She smiled. 'How nice to see you—and Janice! Is Isobel making some supper? I'll go and take over.'

She went out to the kitchen and her clear voice floated back to them.

'I'll do this, Isobel. You'd better go

and rescue Mark!'

Mark's eyes, appalled, met Janice's. Then, seeing that she understood the situation, he gave her a wry smile and continued to chat as Isobel entered. They gave no sign that they had heard, not wanting to upset Isobel any more.

When Mrs Dawson entered with the tray, things went smoothly, and it wasn't until Janice rose to go home that she launched another barb.

'I hear you have yet another string to your bow, Janice.' Her voice was saccharine. 'You're quite a collector, aren't you?'

Janice refrained from any reply but a smile.

'Goodbye, Mrs Dawson,' she said pleasantly. 'Thank you for the supper.'

She turned to Isobel and Mark.

'Do come up for coffee any evening,' she invited. 'I know you don't finish till late, Mark, but neither do I. Remember, I've visited the opposition twice now. It's time you did the same!'

'We'll certainly come up soon,' Mark said, sincerely.

As Isobel saw Janice to her car, they

heard Mrs Dawson speak again.

'Quite a lady of the manor, isn't she?'

Janice turned to Isobel, who looked distressed.

'Don't let that worry you, Isobel. Your mother doesn't worry me.' She paused before continuing softly. 'I do wish I could advise you, Isobel, but I haven't the knowledge. Couldn't you ask your doctor to have a chat with her?'

By the time Janice left, Isobel seemed clearer in her own mind.

The following evening, there was a phone call from Bryan. Janice felt no thrill when she heard his voice and, after the call, she felt gloomy. Things were not becoming any clearer, and she felt content to let things work themselves out.

At the weekend, there was a full house for the first time, and for the first time, too, difficulties appeared. Every weekend till now, the guests had all been skiers and had mixed together happily, regardless of whether they were hotel guests or from the ski-annexe.

This weekend, the annexe had been

booked by the ski-club of a large Edinburgh company. The members were mostly young and casually dressed. The house-guests were mainly skiers, too, the exceptions being a middle-aged man, his wife and his mother. Mr Archibald had been a guest at the hotel the previous autumn and, he told Hugh on arrival, he'd enjoyed the quiet atmosphere on that occasion.

'I'm afraid the atmosphere is a little different now,' Hugh observed when he mentioned it to Janice. 'I hope Mr Archibald isn't too disappointed.'

Janice had ensured that they had a table in the corner farthest from the annexe part of the dining-room. However, at dinner on Friday evening, one of the waiters reported that the Archibalds were looking none too pleased.

'Mr Archibald asked me if we were running a holiday-camp now,' he told Janice. 'When I explained about the ski-annexe, he said that surely they could at least dress for dinner!'

When the meal was over, Ian, the waiter, was able to report that at least the

Archibalds had enjoyed the food. They had also requested early-morning tea, which put Janice in a dilemma. The hotel didn't normally serve early-morning tea, so she decided to make an exception and see to it herself.

The alarm clock woke her at seven o'clock. As she rose to wash and dress, she was struck by the heavy stillness which lay all around. As she opened her curtains to peer out into the darkness, she could see the reason for this. Thick snow lay everywhere.

Janice prepared the tea and juice for the Archibalds, and when she returned from taking this to them, Hugh appeared. Bidding her a brief good-morning, he went to the back passage, where she heard him donning gum boots and going out. Within minutes he returned.

'I'll get the children up,' he said calmly. 'We may need the twins to help this morning. Judging by what I see out there, the service road to the Glen is blocked.'

Janice stared at him, speechless. Full house, and no staff!

'Well,' Hugh continued briskly. 'I'll just check on Jet and call the children. Then I'll take the Land-Rover down the road to see what it's like.'

He hurried out.

Janice's mind began to function again. She organised the breakfasts so they'd need the minimum of attention.

The twins and Robbie arrived down, looking serious and important. After their hands had been well washed, the boys were set to make toast while Mary helped Janice to put finishing touches to the tables.

When Hugh returned he confirmed that the road was blocked, and would remain like that for several hours.

By the time that everyone arrived for breakfast, everything was ready. The annexe guests immediately offered to serve their own, while Janice decided that she would wait at the tables of the house-guests and left Hugh to keep things running smoothly in the kitchen.

Her head was in a whirl by the time the tea-and-toast stage was reached, but all seemed to have gone well, and she and Hugh relaxed a little. Janice took a last look over the tables to see that everyone had all that was needed. Mr Archibald caught her eye, and summoned her over to his table.

'This is just not good enough,' he began.

Janice was surprised, as she couldn't think of any cause for complaint.

'Was something wrong?' she enquired politely.

'Indeed it was!' His voice was raised. 'We are here as a family, and we like to eat as a family. My omelette arrived at this table fully three minutes before the ladies' boiled eggs. Also our toast was brought to the table by a mere child!'

Janice thought of the effort which had gone on in the kitchen to produce their special orders; Hugh, delighted by the texture of the plain omelette he had made, and Paul, timing the boiling of the eggs with intense concentration. And then Mary, the 'mere child,' solemnly bearing the rack of golden toast with careful hands.

'I'm very sorry,' she said. 'As you know, we're snowed up, and none of the staff has managed through.'

'Inefficiency always finds excuses! We should have gone to this new hotel—flashy-looking place, but at least the service will be decent!'

Janice was almost too furious to reply, until she heard herself say, 'Perhaps you should have gone there. You'll know the next time.'

She swung round and left him, his face flushing with anger. As she calmed, she felt very ashamed of herself. However provoked, she ought not to have spoken to a guest in that tone.

Entering the kitchen, she heard Paul call from the panty.

'Come and look. The wee light on the deep-freeze is out.'

Hugh and Janice hurried over.

'There must be a fault in it.' Hugh sounded worried.

Janice lifted the lid and had a quick look, before shutting it again.

'The top's defrosting. It must have been off for some time. Do you know anything about these things?'

'Afraid not.' Hugh's voice was rueful. 'We must do something quickly, though. All the food's at risk now.'

167

'And the road! An engineer won't be able to get through!'

As they stared at each other, the gravity of the situation struck them both. There was hundreds of pounds worth of food in the freezer which had already been off for some hours. Something had to be done soon to save it, for time was running out.

As Hugh and Janice looked helplessly at each other, Janice was remembering the hours that she and Annie Mackay had spent preparing the Christmas fare stored in the faulty freezer. Would all their efforts be wasted as the temperature in the deep-freeze rose past danger point?

'We'll phone the company,' Hugh said. 'They'll advise us how long we've got before the food is spoiled. If the road is opened soon, and they can send an engineer in, perhaps we'll save most of it.'

He hurried out to his office.

'That's all I need you for just now,' Janice told the children who'd been helping her clear away. 'Out you go now and enjoy yourselves. Put plenty of clothes on, remember.'

Joyfully, the children hurried out of the kitchen as their father entered, in a different mood however.

'Not much news, I'm afraid,' he announced. 'I rang the number of the firm, but got through to an answering service. However, it did give a number to ring in case of emergency. This got me to an engineer's home, but his wife answered the phone. She told me her husband was called out earlier this morning and she doesn't know when he'll get back. I left our number and asked her to tell him to contact me whenever he comes in.'

'What about the road?' Janice asked.

'Well, I phoned the County Roads Department. The snow-plough is working in the Glen road at the moment, and they expect to have it clear pretty soon. Then they'll do the side roads. It just depends if they run into any snags; they could be here in an hour, or not till the afternoon.'

Hugh looked in disgust at his hands.

'These,' he said wryly, 'are no good when it comes to mechanical things.

They can draw and paint, but with deep-freezers they're useless!'

'What's so useless?' asked a voice, and on hearing it, Janice and Hugh started with surprise. In the doorway, face glowing with the cold air, was Annie Mackay.

'Annie!' Janice cried. 'How marvellous to see you. But how on earth did you get here? And you're supposed to be off this morning!'

'Och, I thought you'd need a helping hand, maybe. We came over the field on the lee side with the tractor. Donald had to come over to see how the sheep were faring, anyway. I knew that Etta wouldn't manage, so I thought I could make myself useful.'

Janice understood then. Annie, like them, was snowed up from the Glen road, but across the sheltered side of the grazing the snow wouldn't present too many problems for a tractor.

'I'm so pleased to see you!' Janice told her, while Hugh hurried out to have a word with Donald Mackay.

As she made a warm drink for Annie, Janice told her about their worry concerning the freezer. Annie was appalled.

'All the mince-meat and Christmas puddings,' she mourned, 'and the salmon—and steaks! Oh, Miss Taylor, surely it won't all go to waste?'

'I sincerely hope not.'

But Janice wasn't feeling very hopeful as she went upstairs to the residents' lounge to check that the fire was burning brightly. She was a little abashed to find Mr Archibald installed there, reading a magazine. A feeling of shame at her previous loss of temper made her address him impulsively.

'Mr Archibald, I'm very sorry for having spoken rudely to you this morning. I—'

But she got no further. Mr Archibald had sprung to his feet, casting his magazine aside.

'My dear young lady,' he began, 'please don't continue. My womenfolk have told me that I owe you an apology. In fact, I gather that I'm rather out of favour on account of my behaviour at breakfast. Please forgive me.'

Janice was so surprised at this change of face in one who had seemed, only an hour earlier, to be the most ill-tempered of men, that she was at a loss for words. Finally, she smiled.

'That's very generous of you, Mr Archibald. I'm not usually so abrupt with my guests. I suppose that the minor crisis this morning must have upset me more than I realised.'

'And I, too, was not myself.'

Mr Archibald indicated a chair, and Janice sat down, rather unwilling to spare the time on this, the busiest of mornings, but not wishing to spoil this new, friendly relationship. Mr Archibald resumed his seat and began to explain confidentially.

'I have a son. He's had all the advantages I never had. I'm what they call a self-made man—and I'm self-educated, too. No University for me. Just night-school three nights a week after a hard day's work. But I succeeded. I've been able to give my son all the things I couldn't have when I was his age, a good education at a good school, and the promise of a position in the Company after University. But is he grateful?'

Janice could see that Mr Archibald

172

was becoming heated again, but before she could reply he continued:

'Not a bit of it! He told me last week he has no interest in engineering. He wants to be a photographer. He wears his scruffiest clothes although we've never kept him short of money, and he hasn't had a hair cut for a year!'

He shook his head, in sorrow and anger.

Janice was wondering what all this had to do with Kirkton House Hotel, and Mr Archibald's complaints. As if he read her thoughts, her companion gave a short laugh.

'Then I come here, expecting to forget my problems for a few days, and the first thing I saw was a crowd of long-haired, young people who've probably never worked in their lives!'

Janice nodded, slowly.

'I can see that they'd be a red rag to a bull,' she commented, and then was uncomfortably conscious of the aptness of her remark. Mr Archibald did indeed look very bull-like. She hurried on: 'But you're wrong about one thing. All the skiers in the Annexe do have jobs.' She mentioned the name of the Edinburgh Company they all worked for. 'They may have long hair and casual dress, but they're certainly not work-shy. And neither, if I may say so, can your son be, if he's won a place at University. They're hard to come by, these days.'

Mr Archibald looked at her, frowning, and she wondered if she had gone too far. Then his expression changed.

'You may be right,' he said gruffly. 'My wife thinks I'm too hard on the boy.'

Janice, feeling that she really must bring the conversation to a close and continue with her work, rose to her feet.

'You must excuse me, Mr Archibald. There's a lot to be done this morning. To add to our worries, the deep-freeze has broken down. We're just hoping the engineer can get through before all the food is spoiled.'

'Broken down, has it? What seems to be the trouble?'

'Oh, we've no idea. The pilot light is out, and it's beginning to defrost.'

A gleam had come into Mr Archibald's eye.

'Take me to it!' he commanded. 'I'll have a look at it.'

Seeing Janice's surprise, he added, 'Don't look so anxious. I know what I'm doing. I may be a director now, but I pride myself that I know all about the inside of any machine we produce. We make freezers, and one is very much like another. I'll see what I can do.'

Elated, Janice showed him to the machine, where, after requesting a screwdriver, he set to work, jacket off and sleeves rolled up. Hugh stood beside him respectfully, like an apprentice, handing the screwdriver as it was required. Janice left them to it, as she continued with the housework.

Half-an-hour later, she returned to the kitchen to find Mr Archibald sitting at the kitchen table enjoying a cup of tea and talking to Hugh. One look at them told Janice that the deep-freeze was mended. They were in deep discussion about some portable ski-tow apparatus which was lying in an out-house.

'I'm not mechanically minded,' Hugh was confessing. 'I know it ran off a tractor engine, but how, I don't know.'

'Let's have a look at it, lad.'

Mr Archibald rose enthusiastically and the two men departed to view the contraption. After an hour, with Donald Mackay's help, there was a make-shift ski-tow operating on the side of the hill. The skiers, whose spirits had been flagging a little as they climbed upwards for the umpteenth time, took new heart, and were soon going up and down in an endless stream.

Janice was watching the happy, lively scene, when she realised that Hugh was beside her.

'Look at that,' he said, nodding towards a portly figure who was making his way cautiously down the slope, only to sit down with a thud at the bottom.

'Goodness, it's Mr Archibald!'

Janice watched in surprise as he picked himself up, brushed off the loose snow, and joined the short queue for the ski-tow.

'He said he'd always wanted to try,' Hugh explained, 'and so I kitted him out.'

They watched again while their guest descended once more, and this time he stopped successfully, using the snow-plough stop. Seeing them watching, he waved at them happily.

'I think I'm beginning to get the hang of it now. Very exhilarating!'

The two Mrs Archibalds were watching him with a kind of fearful pride.

'Their weekend isn't turning out exactly as planned,' Hugh commented, as he and Janice returned to the kitchen. 'Still, I think they're enjoying it.'

'Isn't it great to see the place so busy? You must feel very pleased that your plans have turned out so well,' Janice remarked, but could have bitten out her tongue when she heard his reply.

'The ski-annexe was Sheila's idea, really. I'm just carrying out what she planned to do.'

He stopped abruptly, turned and left her. Before he went, Janice saw the expression in his eyes. The memory of Sheila must still hurt very much, she thought, blaming herself for being so tactless.

Janice and Annie were just putting the finishing touches to lunch when the snow-plough circled slowly in front of the hotel. Behind it came the post van, and the little car belonging to Ian, one of the young waiters. Out of this jumped the other three waiters, full of apologies for having been unable to come when they should. Not long after this, Etta arrived, too, and things were back to normal.

Lunch was a happy affair. Everyone was ravenous after the morning's exertions. Mr Archibald was in great spirits, and over his coffee began discussing skiing technicalities with the other skiers. He was obviously taking his new sport seriously.

After lunch, almost everyone went to the higher slopes to make the most of the sunny afternoon.

The staff were all happy as they prepared dinners. Only Hugh, when he came in and out, seemed pre-occupied and serious. Janice couldn't help feeling that the remark she made in the morning had stirred up some long repressed feelings and memories of his dead wife.

In the middle of the afternoon, the phone began to ring. It rang several times and Janice, realising that Hugh couldn't be in his office, hurried to answer it. Hugh, however, arrived just in front of her, and picked up the receiver. Janice was about to turn away when she heard him give an exclamation. A quick glance at his face sent her hurrying forward, for it was ashen.

'What's wrong?' she asked anxiously, and Hugh stared at her blankly for a few seconds, then he gave a deep sigh.

'It's all right,' she said, putting a hand to his eyes as he replaced the receiver.

'They just said an accident, and for a moment I thought—'

With obvious effort, he pulled himself together.

'It's Mrs Archibald,' he said, more briskly. 'Her car's stuck. I'll take the Land-Rover and pull them out. She was on her way back up the Glen from Blairochry, with her mother-in-law, when they swerved to avoid another car. They went up on to the banking of snow, and now they're stuck fast.'

He hurried out, and Janice went slowly back to the kitchen, to find that Annie was there by herself. Janice was so puzzled about Hugh's extreme reaction to such a minor mishap that she found herself relating the whole event to Annie. When Janice finished, she looked at her seriously and stopped rolling the pastry she was making.

'Ay,' she said softly, 'he'd get a right shock if they said there was an accident today. I mind, it was a Saturday just a year ago now, when he got the phone call. The police, it was, to tell him that Mrs Murray had crashed the car. There was nothing could be done for her, poor soul. He'd be remembering that, I've no doubt.'

'I see,' Janice said sadly. 'That explains a lot. The whole thing must be very much in his mind these days.'

'Such a bonny lass,' Annie was continuing, as if thinking aloud, 'with her fair hair and her blue eyes. Robbie takes after her. She was aye busy and cheerful, and full of plans. The accident was a cruel blow.'

The others returned to the kitchen, then, and the conversation changed, but Janice thought several times during the evening about what had been said.

The remainder of the weekend was

less eventful, and by Sunday evening all the guests had departed, having enjoyed their stay at Kirkton House. The Archibalds left with many promises to return although Mr Archibald was a little stiff after his unusual exercise.

Later on Sunday evening, there was a phone call from Bryan. He phoned frequently and also wrote to Janice, always looking forward to his stay at the hotel in January. Janice was no nearer sorting out her feelings than she had been the previous week. She was glad to have something to chat about on the phone, and told Bryan about the snow and the deep-freeze. By the time she had finished her story and he had replied with his news, there was little time left for endearments, and Janice rang off, feeling relieved.

She had not seen Sandy since she met him at the Euroscot Hotel, when she was with Bryan. She found herself wishing she could see him and talk to him, but at the same time she was dreading an encounter. No such meeting occurred, however, and she didn't hear any news of him.

CHAPTER 9

During the next week, Hugh and Janice
set off for Dundee, to complete the
Christmas shopping. Janice had told the
children to write their letters to Father
Christmas, giving a list of three choices,
from which 'Santa' would select one.
Robbie took the whole affair very
seriously, watching in wide-eyed wonder
as the smoke from his burning paper
drifted up the chimney.

Janice got the impression that the
twins were reaching the doubtful stage,
but both of them seemed anxious to
believe in the magic of Christmas, and if
they had doubts, they didn't voice them.

Armed with a copy of their lists, Hugh
and Janice set off for Dundee after
breakfast. Janice had been rather
dreading this outing, wondering if the
atmosphere between Hugh and herself
would become strained, as it had done so

often lately. As they drove through the Sidlaws towards the city they talked lightly of general topics, and Janice felt her spirits rise.

She hadn't been on a shopping spree since her Glasgow visit, and she made up her mind to enjoy herself on this outing.

The children had not been greedy, and their requests were all very reasonable. After a toy had been selected for each of them to come from Santa, Janice bought another item on each list to be a present from her.

By the time this was done, it was lunchtime.

'Let's take these things and lock them in the boot, then we'll find some lunch,' Hugh suggested.

As they settled down in the dining-room of a modern hotel, constraint fell upon them. Janice racked her brains to think of something to say which couldn't possibly bring unhappy memories to Hugh, but the more she thought, the less able she was to start a conversation.

Finally, although her voice sounded a little strained as it broke the silence, she asked:

'Have you been doing any drawing lately?'

'I haven't done anything for some time,' Hugh replied. Then he added, with a touch of his former confidence, 'Actually, I had a letter about this very subject yesterday. The chap who did the text for our last book is keen to do another. He wants me to illustrate it, but I doubt if I'll have time to do it. Not if I keep on the hotel.'

Janice nearly choked at this. She had thought, with the initial success of the ski-annexe, that all Hugh's doubts had gone. He must have seen her surprise, for he continued, staring at his plate and avoiding her eyes.

'I was surprised myself how keen I am to do this illustrating work—I didn't know how much I'd missed painting. But with the annexe to run as well as the hotel, there's just not time.

'I often feel that this isn't the best life for the children. I'm so busy when they're on holiday I hardly see them when they most need me. And with there being only me now, I should play a bigger part in their lives.'

184

Janice felt a bit hurt at this. Surely the children were partly her concern, too? Hugh seemed to know what she was thinking, because he looked up at her.

'The children have come to love you,' he said diffidently, 'but that's not the answer. I see that now. They need a lasting relationship. You can go away at any time, after all.

'No, it's my responsibility, and in many ways I've shirked it. It took you to get to the bottom of Mary's anxiety. I should have been able to help her, but I couldn't.'

He stopped speaking, obviously a little embarrassed at having given away so much of what was in his mind. Janice, too, was silent as she thought about what he had said.

'You're right, I suppose,' she said finally. 'I hadn't thought of it like that. Have you definitely decided what you're going to do?'

'No,' Hugh replied, ruefully. 'I'm going to have to think it all through before I make any decision. But you'll be the first to know, I promise you that.'

When they had finished their meal,

Hugh set off in a new direction.

'I always give the children books,' he explained. 'We'll go along the Nethergate to the bookshop.'

They left the modern precinct, and soon were in a different Dundee. As they walked along, Janice looked around at the old buildings.

They had reached the bookshop, and as they both loved books they spent a happy hour browsing around and also choosing the children's Christmas books. When business was completed, Janice had a sudden thought.

'Is any of your work here?' she asked Hugh.

He nodded, and led her to the Natural History Section. He selected a book and handed it to her, open at colour plates in the centre.

'That's it,' he said, casually.

Janice looked at the flower illustrations, meticulously detailed and subtly coloured.

'They're exquisite,' she breathed, overcome with admiration.

Hugh looked boyish and discomfited. He glanced hurriedly at his watch.

'It's about time we were getting back,' he said. 'Have you any more shopping to do?'

On the journey home, both of them were rather silent. Janice was trying to adjust to the idea that Hugh might, after all, sell the hotel. She had resolved, when she took the job at Kirkton House, that she would always remember that she could, at any time, be parted from the children. Now, she realised just how fond of them she had become, and the thought of leaving in the near future was very upsetting, but she knew she had to try and accept it.

Hugh's thoughts must have been running on parallel lines, for he turned to her and asked:

'Do you have any plans for leaving the district soon?'

Janice realised that he was referring to Bryan. He had, after all, seen him on his flying visit North, and knew that he was frequently in touch by phone and letter.

'I have no plans,' she answered, simply. 'None at all.'

'I see,' he answered thoughtfully. 'We both seem to be in the same state of indecision.' He smiled at her.

At least, Janice reflected, Hugh seemed to have got over the effect of Mrs Dawson's remarks to him. They were back on their former, friendlier footing.

'When does your family come from abroad?' she asked.

'In the New Year. They've to find somewhere suitable to live, perhaps on the South coast. I think it's going to be rather difficult. Property prices down there have fairly rocketed in the last year.'

They arrived back at Kirkton House and managed to stow the parcels away before collecting the children from school. Janice felt a thrill of anticipation as she imagined their joy on Christmas morning.

Whatever else, Hugh must be free to give his children full attention on that special day.

Janice was pleased to have a phone call that evening from Isobel.

'Mark and I thought of calling in later. Would it be suitable?' she asked.

'Of course. It will be lovely to see you

both. Come when you can.'

Janice mentioned the visit to Hugh.

'I'll take them to the residents' lounge,' she said, 'since we have no-one in tonight.'

'May I join you later?' Hugh asked. 'I liked what I saw of Mark Proctor. I could show him round.'

'I'm sure he'd like that,' Janice nodded.

When her visitors arrived around nine o'clock, Janice had them to herself for a while. She noticed at once that Isobel was looking very happy, and was not surprised when she announced that she had some news.

Janice's eyes went involuntarily to Isobel's left hand, but it was still ringless. The news must be something different.

'It's mother!' Isobel explained. 'She's had a letter from the television company. She's to meet one of their producers, with a view to being a guest on Frank Dale's programme!'

'How marvellous!' Janice said. 'When does she go?'

'It's next week. But Janice, you've no idea what a change this has made! She's so happy, and not spiteful at all. She even mentioned that she knew she had been rude to you several times, and was sorry about it. I can't tell you what a load has gone from my mind.'

She turned to Mark. 'Isn't she much better?' she appealed.

'She's quite a different person,' Mark agreed, smiling at the girl by his side.

It was very clear how he felt about Isobel. Janice, too, was happy at her friends relief. If she had doubts about Mrs Dawson's sudden change of personality, she kept them to herself.

The three of them chatted pleasantly, Janice recounting the story of their eventful weekend at Kirkton House. She had just risen to fetch the supper when Hugh appeared. He took Isobel and Mark on a tour of the hotel and the annexe while Janice was busy in the kitchen.

Janice wondered how Isobel was feeling, touring her former home like that. Every corner of the house must be full of childhood memories and reminders of a way of life which was no longer hers. Mark also would be doubly interested in Kirkton House; he would see it not only through his professional eye as a rival hotel, but also as the former home of the girl he loved.

If Isobel had been thinking along these lines, she didn't betray her thoughts. She was enthusiastic about the changes which had been made in the house and very impressed by the ski-annexe, and over supper the only reference she made to the past was to say how glad she was that the atmosphere of the house hadn't been spoiled. Mark shared her point of view.

'It's a lovely country-house type of atmosphere,' he said. 'It's fine that it has been retained.'

Janice noticed that Hugh and Isobel were much easier with each other than on former meetings. Perhaps Isobel's obvious acceptance of Kirkton House as it now was had helped Hugh to see that she didn't share her mother's obsession about the house. There was no bitterness in Isobel's manner. She obviously didn't feel that she had been 'cheated of her birthright,' as her mother had so dramatically put it.

Mark's easy manner contributed to the happy atmosphere of the visit, and

Hugh's first impressions were obviously being confirmed, as he and Mark found plenty to talk about.

As Mark and Isobel left, Janice referred to Mrs Dawson again.

'Wish your mother the best of luck from me,' Janice told Isobel. 'I'm sure she'll do well. Her voice is so lovely and she has such a striking appearance.'

At this, of course, Hugh had to be put in the picture. As Mark and Janice watched Isobel's happy face explaining the situation to Hugh, Mark spoke quietly to Janice.

'Let's hope she's not disappointed. I dread to think what will happen if nothing comes of this.'

Janice nodded, in full agreement. He had put into words the doubts which loomed large in her own mind. Whether Isobel shared these doubts and was merely refusing to recognise their existence, Janice couldn't know. As she waved her friend off, she fervently hoped that her happy relief would not prove ill-founded.

Every morning, the children took Jet for a run before school. He was well established as a member of the family, and now came to heel at once when called. The morning after Isobel's visit, they set out as usual. It was a dull morning, almost dark. Much of the snow had gone from around the hotel, and as the children and dog made their way briskly along the side of the dyke Janice could just make out their moving figures as she looked from the bright kitchen.

She had moved away from the window to busy herself in another part of the kitchen when there was a commotion at the back door, and Paul burst in to the room, wild and pale.

'It's Jet!' he gasped. 'Something's choking him. Please come!'

Janice ran after Paul, heedless of the damp which soaked her indoor shoes. Jet lay on the ground, Mary and Robbie crouching with terrified faces, by his side. The dog was in great distress, making painful choking noises.

'What happened?'

'I think he tried to eat something he found.' Mary's voice was trembling. 'What shall we do?'

'Paul! Run and fetch your father.

Mary and Robbie, stay with Jet, I'll phone the vet.'

Janice ran back to the hotel and, with trembling fingers, dialled the number. So great was her concern for Jet that it wasn't until she heard the number ring that she realised Sandy might reply. But it was another voice which answered the phone; Bob Aitken, Sandy's partner.

'Please come quickly to Kirkton House Hotel.' Janice was breathless from running. 'It's the Labrador, Jet, he seems to have something stuck in his throat, and he's bleeding from the mouth.'

'I'll be there right away.'

Janice hurried out to see Hugh carrying Jet in his arms to an outhouse.

'Get his blanket and bring it here,' he instructed Mary.

Soon Jet, still making dreadful gutteral noises, was lying on the blanket on a workbench, which was well lit from above.

There was nothing to do now but wait.

'I'll go round and meet the vet, and show him where to come,' Janice suggested.

No-one answered. All attention was concentrated on that pitiful black figure on the table.

Janice waited tensely at the side of the hotel until, with a screech of brakes, a Land-Rover drew up and a man jumped out.

'Mr Aitken,' she began. 'Thank goodness you're here—'

Then she saw it was Sandy. He didn't even look at her.

'Where's Jet?' he demanded brusquely, brushing past her.

Surprise at Sandy's unexpected appearance struck Janice speechless for a few seconds until Sandy turned back to her.

'Where is he?' he asked again, impatiently. 'Every minute matters.'

Janice hurried forward then, leading him silently to the outhouse. The little group round the gasping body moved back to let Sandy examine his patient.

'Mr Nicol will help Jet now,' Hugh gently told the children. 'Come away, and give him room to work.'

Unprotesting, their faces still drawn and shocked, the children allowed themselves to be shepherded back to the hotel. Janice hovered at the door, uncertain whether to go or stay.

'Here, hold Jet's head.'

Sandy's voice brooked no argument, and Janice did as she was told. She held Jet's head, while Sandy, with his jacket off and his sleeves rolled up, worked swiftly and skilfully, occasionally issuing some command: 'Hold the torch here,' he would say, or 'Swab, quickly!'

Soon, there lay on the table several splinters of bone, some tiny, but one large enough to have spanned Jet's throat.

'Chicken bones,' Sandy commented. 'Never give these to a dog!'

From his tone, Janice knew he thought the offending bones had been given as food to Jet, but this wasn't the time to explain.

'I think he'll do now. He's had a bad time, but he'll recover in a day or two.

'I'll give him an antibiotic shot which should counteract any infection.'

Having done this, he stroked Jet's black head, to be rewarded by a feeble thump of tail on table. Sandy gathered the limp body into his arms.

'I'll take him to his basket,' he said. 'Then I'd appreciate a wash.'

For the first time, he looked at Janice.

'Thanks for your help,' he said. 'You don't flap, do you?'

Such praise brought a sudden flush to Janice's cheeks, and she was glad that Sandy had moved away with Jet. Quickly she made her way back to the hotel kitchen, where four anxious faces turned to greet her.

'Mr Nicol's finished,' she told them, 'and I think you could have a peep at Jet, if you're very quiet.'

Three very relieved children rushed out to see their dog. Janice explained the situation to Hugh, then noticed the time.

'Goodness!' she exclaimed. 'The children are late for school!'

'I know,' Hugh confessed. 'I just hadn't the heart to take them down before knowing the news about Jet. They'd have been utterly miserable.'

'I'll take them now,' Janice volunteered. She knew she was avoiding being alone with Sandy again, but she couldn't help it. He roused such powerful emotions in her that, in the uncertainty

197

of her mind, her reaction was to keep out of his way.

'Sandy says he needs a wash,' she remembered.

'And I'll make some coffee,' Hugh said.

Janice called the children and drove the happy cargo to school. They were quite light-hearted with relief, and giggled for most of the journey.

She explained briefly the reason for their late arrival to Isobel, before returning to the hotel, where she found Sandy sitting at the kitchen table, coffee, toast and an omelette before him.

'I discovered that this man rushed out with no breakfast,' Hugh explained, 'so I just rustled up something for him.'

'It was your partner who answered the phone,' Janice told Sandy, trying to converse normally.

'Yes, I was just coming downstairs. When I heard it was Jet, I had to come. He knows me.'

Just then, the phone rang, and Hugh went to answer it. Janice was very conscious of being alone with Sandy. He, however, continued calmly with his breakfast, finishing his omelette before speaking.

'How did Jet get hold of those bones? They're lethal for a dog.'

'I've no idea,' she replied stiffly. 'Mary just said he found something outside and tried to eat it. But how chicken bones would come to be lying at the bottom dyke, I've no idea.'

There was silence for a while, until Sandy, not looking at Janice, remarked casually:

'I hear changes are in the air at Kirkton House.'

Janice stared at him, surprised, and he suddenly raised his head and looked straight into her eyes. Their glances locked for an endless moment, in which, for Janice, the whole world was contained in two piercing grey eyes.

It was Sandy who looked away first and, when he spoke, his voice was husky.

'We'll miss you,' he said.

At that moment, Hugh returned, seeming unconscious of the tension in the room. When, soon after this, Sandy rose to leave, it was Hugh who walked with him to the car, giving Janice and Sandy no opportunity for further conversation.

When Sandy had gone, Janice's brain began to function again. What on earth had he meant by his remark?

Suddenly, she thought she knew. Hugh must, in their time alone, have told Sandy that he intended to sell the hotel. He must finally have come to a decision about his family's future.

But he promised I'd be the first to know! she protested to herself. Surely he could have told me before telling Sandy. After all, it's my future that's at stake!

By the time that Hugh returned, she had worked herself into a state of indignation—quite justified indignation, she persuaded herself.

'Jet's asleep,' Hugh announced. 'I can't thank Sandy enough for coming so quickly.'

He did not seem to notice that Janice's reply was in distinctly huffy tones, and continued to chat for a few minutes about the healthy state of bookings. Finally, he became aware of Janice's frosty replies.

'Is something wrong?' he enquired.

'Nothing at all,' she replied airily. 'I

200

just thought you might have some more important news to tell me.'

'News?' Hugh sounded genuinely puzzled. 'What news do you mean?'

As Hugh stared at her, utterly at a loss, doubts began to creep into Janice's mind. Could she have jumped too quickly to conclusions, a fault she'd accused Hugh of having done not so very long ago?

'At least,' she added lamely, 'Sandy said there were changes in the air here, and I took it you'd made your decision to leave Kirkton.'

'I have made no decision yet, and when I do, you will be the first to know. I promised that before, didn't I?'

Janice felt very ashamed of her hasty words.

'I think Sandy was referring to your future plans, not mine.'

'My plans?' Janice was astounded.

'It seems that he heard you were going back to London soon. Presumably to be with your friend there. He asked me if it were true, but I couldn't confirm or deny the rumour.'

'Going back to London? Who could have told him that?' Janice asked. Now she was genuinely puzzled.

'I gathered it was Isobel Dawson.'

'Isobel! Why would she tell Sandy a thing like that? I certainly never told her that I was thinking of leaving.'

'I did think it a bit odd,' Hugh went on, 'after your assuring me that you had no plans. I thought things must have changed since last week.'

'Well, they haven't. Anyway, if they do, I promise, you'll be the first to know!'

Janice, when she thought about this conversation, felt rather hurt. Why should Isobel mislead Sandy into thinking she was going to London to be with Bryan?

There must be some mistake, she told herself.

But why did it matter what Sandy thought? She remembered again the look he had given her, the tone of his voice when he told her that she would be missed. Was she deceiving herself when she thought that these things proved she mattered to Sandy?

And Bryan—surely it was time she sorted out her feelings about Bryan.

Her thinking was interrupted by Hugh, who brought her a letter which had arrived by the post van. It was from Bryan, and Janice took it to her room to read it.

After she had read to the end she sat for a while staring at the bold handwriting, completely stunned. The letter was not long, but at the end it posed a question: would Janice accept an engagement ring for Christmas?

Her violent reaction took her by surprise. One emotion flooded through her, and this was panic.

I can't, she thought wildly. I can't get engaged to Bryan! Not at Christmas. Not ever.

The warm affection she felt for him was no basis for marriage, when a mere glance from another man could thrill her senses in a way that Bryan's kisses had never done.

After she'd decided to phone Bryan in the evening, she made an effort to compose herself before returning downstairs.

That afternoon, Janice was off duty, so she set off for the slopes. She took the first run slowly. It was two years since she had been on skis and it took a little time to get the feel of them again. As she neared the bottom, skill and confidence began to return and she managed a couple of tight parallel turns before stopping neatly at the foot of the slope.

'Very nice, Janice!' a voice called, and there was Mark Proctor.

'Hello, Mark! Are you having a break from the hotel too? Isn't it marvellous?'

'Yes. Marvellous weather for Scotland in December! Long may it last.'

Just then, Mark was joined by an attractive girl. She was tall and blonde, and in her ski outfit she could have stepped straight out of a glossy magazine. Her flared trousers were without a wrinkle and her white anorak was trimmed with fox-fur.

'Oh, Trudi,' Mark said. 'I'd like you to meet Janice Taylor, from Kirkton House Hotel. Janice, this is Trudi Traub. She's come all the way from Switzerland to ski in Scotland!'

They all laughed.

'Are you going up again?' Mark nodded towards the ski lift, and soon the three of them were travelling upwards again.

If Janice had thought Trudi's outfit more suited to a fashion show than to a Scottish ski-slope, she was left in no doubt as to Trudi's ski-ing ability.She was off, flying and swooping like a bird, before Janice had organised herself to start.

Mark also was staring after Trudi in admiration.

'She's away out of my class!' he confided in a tone of regret as he set out a little cautiously for the bottom.

Janice suddenly hoped fervently that the regret in his voice applied only to ski-ing prowess. It would be easy to understand why a man had lost his head over her. Then Janice was reassured when she remembered how Mark looked at Isobel.

The rest of the afternoon flew past and, as early dusk began to fall, Janice headed for home. As she arrived once more at the hotel, her spirits were high. Bryan would understand, she assured herself. A phone call would solve that problem.

She hadn't reckoned on that single-minded tenacity which had made Bryan so successful.

'Janice,' he said, in a reasonable voice, as if talking to a fractious child, 'I think you're just confused. I was wrong to rush you like that, and I'm sorry. Don't be hasty, darling. I'll see you in January and I'm sure things will work out for us.'

'But Bryan, I know they can't! I think we should stop seeing each other.'

'We can hardly do that! We're not seeing each other as it is, and I think that's the root of the trouble. I just wish I could be with you now. I'm sure you'd think differently. Give me a chance, Janice. It can't do any harm to see me again and find out how you feel.'

Janice felt her resolution fade away in the face of this argument. Weakly, she heard herself agreeing and, when she had rung off, she realised resentfully that the position was exactly as it had been before the letter had arrived that morning. She was no nearer resolving her problems.

Well, she thought, I can't stop him coming here for his holiday. Perhaps he'll see for himself how I feel when he arrives in January.

When she gave it a thought, it was amazing how she managed to push Bryan to the back of her mind. For the next day or two she was busy tending Jet, and also with preparations for Christmas in the hotel and for the Murray family.

The week before Christmas Janice collected the children and took them straight from school to Blairochry to do their Christmas shopping.

As Janice drove down the Glen, they met a car coming the opposite way. It was a large car of foreign make and was being driven skilfully, even if rather too fast, for a country road. Janice had just time to make out that the driver was Trudi Traub, with Mark Proctor at her side. At the sight, disquiet again stirred within her. Mark seemed to be spending much of his time off with the lovely Swiss girl.

Shopping with the three was a complicated affair, and Janice had to keep Robbie engrossed in one shop while the twins hurried away to buy his little gifts, or to detain Mary while the boys attended to business at another. For their father's present, they had decided to club together and buy slippers. Here, real difficulties occurred.

'I like these red ones best. They're nice and cosy looking,' Robbie decided, pointing to a pair of carpet slippers.

'Och, those are for an old man! Dad's not very old yet!' Mary protested. 'These leather ones are far smarter, aren't they, Miss Janice?'

'But look, these are super!' Paul was pointing to huge deerskin après-ski bootees. 'Let's get these!'

Obviously it was time for Janice to intervene. Paul's choice had to be eliminated at once, as they were far too expensive.

'Leather ones would be more practical than these carpet slippers, Robbie,' she pointed out, persuasively. 'If Daddy had to go out to the car to fetch something, he wouldn't need to change.'

Robbie still looked rebellious.

'Brown's a boring colour,' he said, disgustedly.

'Shall we see if they have the leather ones in red?' Janice suggested and, luckily, they had managed to find the right thing.

Everyone was very satisfied with the purchase.

When everything was settled, the three had a long discussion before asking Janice if she'd mind waiting where she was while they did a 'private message.'

Fifteen minutes later, when Janice was becoming anxious as well as cold, they came running up, Mary clutching something behind her back.

As the three sang carols all the way back to the hotel, Janice reflected she hadn't spent Christmas with children for many years, and decided she looked forward keenly to the experience.

Even if she hadn't caught the Christmas mood that afternoon, she certainly would have done so the following day, when the children of Kirkton School presented a Nativity Play for parents and friends.

Janice and Hugh had both promised to be present, as the play would last only an hour or so. However, just as Janice and Hugh were about to leave the school, a salesman whom Hugh had been keen to see arrived at the hotel.

'You go on,' Hugh told Janice

hurriedly. 'I'll come when I can.'

'Do try and hurry,' she said, impulsively. 'The children are counting on your being there.'

'Naturally I'll be as quick as I can.' Hugh's tone was stiff.

Janice hurried off, reproaching herself for being unfair. Hugh was all too conscious of how these claims on his time prevented him being with his children on occasions like this and he hardly needed her to remind him. This was the very fact which was causing him to consider changing his whole way of life, to let him have more time to devote to his family.

When Janice arrived at the village hall, where the play was to be presented, there was already quite a crowd of parents and friends in the hall. She was just seated when Isobel appeared from behind the scenes. She smiled at the company and seated herself at the piano, which stood below the stage. As she began to play, the sound of children's voices singing was heard from behind the curtain which slowly opened to reveal the simple set.

The main parts were, of course, played by the older children, but Mary made a sweet angel, Paul a dignified King, and Robbie a sturdy, earnest shepherd. The youngest player there was the Baby Jesus. Instead of using a doll, the girl who played Mary had "borrowed" her own little brother, who lay beaming and coo-ing in the manger, waving tight chubby fists in the air and bringing a tear to many an eye.

It wasn't until just before the curtains closed that Janice at last saw Hugh tip-toeing hurriedly to his seat. She saw too that this late arrival had not escaped the sharp eyes of the children.

When the closing tableau had been formed and the whole company had joined in "Away in a Manger," the curtain closed to the hearty applause of the audience.

Very impressed comments came from all around. Isobel, looking pleased and flushed, hurried back stage to assist the little actors.

Janice made her way to Hugh, who was looking regretful and rather abashed.

'I really tried to get away,' he said defensively before she could speak. 'I had just completed business with the sales rep. when I got an important phone call. Are the children upset?'

'I haven't seen them yet,' Janice answered, 'but I think they're bound to be a bit disappointed. They set such store by your presence.'

'But at least you were there for the whole of it.'

'I'm no substitute for you, Hugh. You admitted that yourself the other day,' Janice reminded him.

Just then, the children appeared in their normal clothes once more. They came up to Janice and Hugh but, with one accord, ignored their father and addressed Janice.

'Was it good, Miss Janice?'

'Which bit did you like best?'

'Did I sing out really good?'

'It was splendid,' Janice assured them. 'You all did very well indeed.'

Hugh's voice was heard, sounding a little uncertain.

'I'm really sorry, all of you. I was held up. You see—'

But Mary broke in coolly:

'That's all right. I don't expect you

were really interested in a children's play.'

'Business is more important,' Paul put in.

'Miss Janice came all right,' Robbie added.

Hugh looked relieved that the children were so offhand about his absence. He obviously thought that it wasn't, after all, important to them, but with more intuition Janice suspected that the children had been so hurt that they couldn't admit it.

'May we go and see Hamish's new kittens?' Mary asked. 'His mum says she'll bring us home at five o'clock.'

When Janice had checked with Hamish's mother, the children ran off excitedly, laughing and talking.

'See, they didn't mind my being late one little bit?' Hugh said. 'How we adults worry about nothing!'

Janice made no comment. Perhaps, after all, she had been wrong. She certainly hoped so.

Having seen all her charges safely dressed in their own clothes, Isobel appeared, to mingle with the home-going parents. As she watched her friend, Janice knew that she just couldn't believe that Isobel would maliciously mislead Sandy about her feelings and her future plans.

Janice resolved to talk to her about it, knowing there must be some simple explanation.

Aloud, she said to Hugh, 'I think I'll have a word with Isobel, if you'll excuse me, I'll be up before long.'

When Hugh went off, Janice went over to Isobel, who was now tidying up.

'That was really lovely, Isobel,' she said sincerely. 'You must've worked awfully hard.'

'Oh, the children are all naturals on stage,' Isobel said modestly. 'They love to act and sing, so it wasn't so difficult to train them.

'Have you a minute to spare? I'm dying for a cup of tea.'

They made their way together back to the schoolhouse. When both of them were relaxing, cups in hands, Janice plunged in.

'Isobel, did you tell Sandy that I was leaving Kirkton and going back to

London? He told Hugh that he'd heard this, and Hugh gathered that it was from you.'

Isobel looked genuinely puzzled.

'I didn't tell him. I didn't even know! Are you going back to London?'

'No, I'm certainly not! Where can he have got such an idea?'

Suddenly Isobel put down her cup with a bang.

'I remember now,' she said slowly. 'He asked about Bryan—who he was. It was after he saw you at the new hotel. I told him that he'd come up from London to see you, and Mother made some remark about him being very keen to drive all that way. But I certainly didn't say anything about you going away—'

Suddenly Isobel's voice tailed off, as she remembered something.

'I went to make coffee just then,' she said, frowning. 'Unless Mother said something...' Their eyes met. The mystery was solved.

'Oh, well,' said Janice, sorry for her friend's obvious embarrassment. 'It's not important, I suppose. How is your mother these days? Is she still on top of

215

the world?'

Isobel's face grew even more gloomy.

'Quite the reverse, I'm afraid. She attended the audition, and felt that she'd done well and they liked her. She came back very happy, but they're slower in getting in touch than she expected. For the past few days she's been really depressed. It's so awful, when only last week she was so happy. I really hoped she'd changed.'

Isobel looked down at her cup, her usually bright face sad and worried. Janice sought a subject to cheer her up.

'How's Mark, these days?'

Immediately the words were out, Janice knew she'd made a mistake. It was as if a shutter closed over Isobel's face.

'I don't know,' she said. 'I haven't seen him for the past few days.'

Suddenly, Janice had a vivid picture in her mind of a fast car, driven by a beautiful girl, with Mark by her side. The phrases which had risen to her lips, about how busy Mark would be these days in the hotel died there before she uttered them. She couldn't be insincere with Isobel, as she suspected that it wasn't altogether business which was keeping Mark occupied these days.

Isobel was talking again, her voice expressionless.

'We had a silly quarrel. I suppose I was jealous, really. I'd heard from a few people that he was being seen around a lot with Herr Traub's daughter, Trudi. Have you seen her, Janice? They say she's beautiful. Well, Mark phoned to say he was sorry he hadn't called in to see me for a few days and started telling me about Trudi, and he sounded so friendly with her. Anyway, I was really offhand with him, and that made him upset and we said a lot of things we didn't really mean. At least, I didn't mean them. That was two days ago, and I haven't heard from him since.'

Isobel's voice tailed off.

Before Janice could say anything to her, the door-bell rang. Isobel rose, pushing back her hair with a nervous gesture as she went to open the door.

Janice gave a start of surprise when she recognised the voices, and into the room walked Mark and Trudi Traub.

As Mark and Trudi entered the school-house sitting-room, Janice tried to wipe the astonished expression from her face. A quick glance at Isobel told her that she was not alone in her surprise. Mark looked less relaxed than usual, and in fact the only person who seemed completely un-selfconscious was Trudi. She turned impulsively to Isobel as they were introduced, clasping her hands.

'I am so delighted to meet you, Eesobel,' she said charmingly. 'Mark has told me so many things about you.'

She looked lovely, in black trousers topped by a cuddly cream furry sweater. Isobel pushed back the straying strand of hair again, and Janice knew she was conscious of her slightly dishevelled appearance and work-a-day clothes. She replied, however, in the friendliest of tones, inviting her unexpected guests to sit down, and offering them tea.

Janice realised that it was high time she returned to Kirkton House, and rose to go.

'Oh, must you really go, Janice?' Trudi sounded really regretful. 'Just when we had so nice a party!'

Janice made her excuses, and left. As she drove home, she puzzled over what she'd witnessed. Was Mark trying to demonstrate to Isobel that Trudi was just a friend, whom he wanted to be Isobel's friend too? Or had the visit been Trudi's idea, to give her the chance to weigh up her rival? If so, Trudi must indeed be ruthless. And Mark's attitude, Janice reflected, could hardly have assured Isobel of his feelings for her. He had scarcely looked in her direction during the time that Janice was present.

As she reached the Hotel, Janice felt rather guilty, as she had stayed away longer than she had meant to do. She hurried in, to find the children already home, and Annie serving up their meal.

'Sorry,' Janice said. 'I should be doing that.'

'Och, that's all right,' Annie replied. 'I've just been hearing all about this fine play you've been to. I'm really sorry I missed it.'

Janice noticed that Hugh was frowning at his plate, and wondered if the children had mentioned his absence. She wasn't left in doubt as to their feelings for long though.

'You should have come, Annie. You could have had Dad's seat. He didn't bother to come till the very end,' Mary told Annie.

Hugh laid down his fork.

'Now, children,' he began quietly. 'I've said I'm sorry and I've explained why I was so late.

'I don't want to hear any more about it.' The children all looked sulkily at their father, then Janice, before returning their attention to their food.

The adults pointedly ignored their sulky expressions, chatting lightly together, but Janice was very glad when the meal was over and so, she felt sure, was Hugh. He excused himself from the table and disappeared into his office.

When Janice went to bid the children goodnight, Robbie asked coaxingly:

'Have you time for a story, Miss Janice?'

She knew that from the next day there would be little time to spare for such things. The temporary staff all began then, in preparation for the Christmas House Party, which would arrive on

Christmas Eve.

'I'd like Cinderella,' Paul said. 'We saw a bit of it on television. It was a pantomime.'

The other two agreed, and Janice began the tale. The rapt expressions and wide eyes of her audience inspired her to great dramatic effect and when at last the tale was told there was a sigh of satisfaction from the three.

'That was great,' Mary breathed.

'The step-mother was the horriblest person I ever heard about,' Robbie said solemnly.

As Janice tucked Mary into bed, the little girl looked up at her thoughtfully.

'Are all step-mothers wicked?'

'Good gracious, no!' Janice replied. 'There are lots of nice, kind step-mothers who love the children very much—just as if they were their very own.'

'If Daddy got married again, we'd have a step-mother, wouldn't we?'

'What if she was horrid like the one in the story!' Robbie said, horrified at the thought.

'Don't be daft,' Paul broke in sensibly. 'Dad would never choose someone like that. He'd go for someone nice—like Miss Janice, maybe!'

Three pairs of eyes turned on Janice, who suddenly became very brisk, tucking-in energetically and plumping pillows.

'No more talking now,' she said bracingly. 'It's getting late!'

As she left the children's room she was smiling to herself a little. The thought which had occurred to all of them at once had been obvious, and Janice was heartily glad that Hugh wasn't present at that particular moment.

Next day, the post brought a letter from Jack. Janice's friend who was now a gym teacher in Glasgow, confirming his plans for bringing a school party to the ski-annexe during the third week of January.

'We had some difficulty in finding another qualified leader for the group,' the letter continued. 'However, Grandma turned up trumps by offering to keep the offspring for a week, to let my wife, Kate, come along. As you know, she was a gym teacher too, and we're both thrilled about getting away together to Kirkton. The children are all very enthusiastic about learning to ski and we are all attending dry-ski instruction on the artificial ski-slope in Glasgow.'

Hugh and Janice were pleased about this booking. If the week proved a success, other schools would become interested and the ski-annexe could be fully utilised during the weeks of the school terms, as well as at holiday periods and weekends.

It was a very hectic day. The four schoolboys arrived in the morning and their duties and free-time were worked out. Annie and Etta were busy preparing the stuffings for the turkeys, and other Christmas fare. The children were on holiday from school now and spent much of the day out-of-doors with Jet. In the evening, the tall Christmas tree was erected in the lounge and Hugh and the children decorated it and the rest of the hotel.

CHAPTER 10

Janice prepared next day, Christmas Eve, for the arrival of the members of the house party. The party was all one family, now widely scattered in their homes and jobs, but re-uniting for the Golden Wedding of Mr and Mrs Reid of Blairochry which fell at the Christmas season. They came from many parts of the British Isles, while the eldest son had flown with his wife and family all the way from New Zealand. The re-union had been arranged by the eldest daughter and her husband, a wealthy local farmer. They were the couple who had been so favourably impressed by the food and the atmosphere at Kirkton House that they had booked the whole hotel over Christmas.

As Janice escorted the couple who had organised the party to their rooms, they remarked admiringly on the festive appearance of the hotel.

'It's so gracious and yet so homely, too!' Mrs Rankin enthused. 'And to think we have it all to ourselves!'

She turned to Janice impulsively.

'I'm so excited,' she confided. 'It's the thought of seeing all the family again. We haven't been together like this for over twenty years. There are six of us—three brothers and three sisters—and we've all been spared to see our parents' Golden Wedding. I wrote to them all and said that if we didn't make the effort this time, next year might be too late! And they're all coming, even Bob from New Zealand!'

'Now, now, Nan,' said her husband soothingly, 'come and have a quiet time for a while, till the others arrive.'

As Janice left them, she reflected that an emotional time lay ahead, as each member of the family returned to the fold. When the guests of honour arrived a little later, however, this white-haired couple were serene and unperturbed as their great reunion approached. During the afternoon, they held court in the Residents' Lounge.

Just before dinner, the Glasgow ski-club, who had booked the annexe over Christmas, drove up in their many cars. Their gay voices rang out as they unloaded their gear, and Mrs Rankin, dressing for dinner, must have heard them from her room.

'Who are all these people arriving?' she asked.

'It's a Glasgow ski-club,' Janice was puzzled.

'But I understood that we had booked the whole place,' Mrs Rankin said, her voice full of disappointment.

'They aren't in the actual Hotel,' Janice explained. 'We have a ski-annexe at the back, you see. I don't think they'll trouble you at all.'

Mrs Rankin's brow cleared.

'That's not so bad,' she conceded. 'I suppose they'll be quite self-contained out there.'

'As a matter of fact,' Janice knew her voice sounded apologetic, 'they do share the dining-room. But it's a large L-shaped room, so there should be no difficulty.'

Mrs Rankin looked far from convinced.

226

There was nothing Janice could do. She felt saddened that this misunderstanding had arisen and fervently hoped that the happy atmosphere wouldn't be spoiled in any way. As she worked in the kitchen, helping Etta serve the dinner, she was re-assured by the reports brought back by the waiters from the dining-room.

'They're all raving about that Cock-a-leekie soup,' Iain who was serving the Reids reported. 'But I can see this meal lasting for hours! They're all gabbling as if they haven't seen one another for years.'

Janice, smiling, explained that, in fact, they had not!

The boys who were serving the ski-annexe people were taking in the coffee before the house-party had completed the main course. The skiers were keen to be off. Mark had 'phoned Hugh to invite any of the Kirkton guests to a Christmas Eve Dance in the Euroscot Hotel, and his invitation had been eagerly accepted by the young folk.

'At least,' thought Janice, 'the Reids will have the place to themselves this evening.'

The meal completed at last, the house-party made their way to the residents' lounge. As Janice passed through the hall, four young people from the party, who had hung behind the rest, approached her diffidently.

'Can you tell us, please, where the dance is tonight?' asked a tall youth with an accent which Janice guessed to be New Zealand. 'We heard some of the others talking about it.' He would be a grandson of the Reids, she thought, as she answered his question.

'It's at the new Euroscot Hotel,' she explained. 'It's about a mile farther up the Glen Road. You go down to the junction and turn right. You'll see the sign.'

'Can anyone go?' one of the three girls asked, her voice eager.

'If you're staying here, you've been invited,' Janice assured her. 'Just explain that you're from Kirkton House.'

Janice went on out to her car. Conveniently, the children had been invited out to tea this evening, and she was going to bring them home.

The children had last-minute wrapping to do, but were pleased to complete it quickly and get away to bed. Hugh also came to supervise the hanging-up of stockings and, having set the children's alarm clock for 7 a.m., they left the trio with strict instructions that they mustn't rise before that hour in the morning.

When Hugh and Janice came downstairs, Hugh left her, to go and speak to his guests in the lounge. Janice continued on to the kitchen to find the dinner things cleared up and preparations well ahead for the Christmas Dinner next day. The guests would have theirs mid-day, and in the evening, the staff would enjoy theirs, served by Hugh and Janice.

Iain and the other three waiters had completed the setting-up of the dining-room for breakfast, and were planning to go to the dance.

'Remember we've a busy day tomorrow,' Janice warned. 'Keep some of your energy for then!'

'You should be coming with us, Miss Taylor,' Iain said, grinning. 'I bet you do a braw Broon's Reel!'

He seized her and spun her round till

she was breathless with exertion and laughter, while the rest clapped. She felt very foolish when she realised that Hugh had entered and was watching her, especially as his face was serious.

'Away you go, all of you!' she gasped. 'Have a good time.'

A little chastened by Hugh's expression, the boys and Etta left. Hugh turned to Janice, who was trying to regain her composure.

'We've had a complaint,' he told her seriously, 'and I feel I'm very much to blame.'

'Was it Mrs Rankin?' Janice asked. 'She mentioned to me that she hadn't expected other guests to be using the dining-room.'

'I just didn't think of mentioning the ski-annexe to her when she made the booking in November. It didn't occur to me that it could make any difference.

'Now, some of the younger relations have gone away to the dance, and she's quite upset about it.'

'What do the others think?' Janice asked.

'Oh, they all seem happy enough and

are having a good old session of the "do-you-remembers." But it was Mrs Rankin who made the booking, and she followed me out of the lounge to express her disappointment. I apologised, of course, but there's nothing else I can do about it.'

'Well, Hugh,' Janice said sensibly, 'you did show her round the hotel, and she must have seen the seating capacity of the dining-room. Even if we hadn't a ski-annexe, we'd have been filling these tables at this time of year. I don't think she has any cause for complaint, really.'

'I didn't think of that.' Hugh looked thoughtful. 'However, I wish it hadn't happened.'

He paused, then added in a different tone:

'When would it be best for Santa to call on the children, do you think?'

'I'd leave it as late as possible,' Janice advised. 'Till they're deeply asleep. I'll help you slip the parcels in. There's a lot!'

Later when Janice wheeled the prepared supper-trolley to the lounge and poured out the tea, there was no hint of dissatisfaction in the manner of the company, as they exclaimed over Annie's baking. In fact, as Janice passed her a plate, Mrs Reid patted her arm gently.

'Everything's just lovely,' she said, smiling at Janice. 'This grand room and the cheery fire and all our bairns gathered around us again. Just lovely.'

And her husband nodded his agreement.

Janice told Hugh about this when she returned to the kitchen.

'At least the guests of honour have no complaint,' she assured him.

He nodded, but added seriously:

'This could be the big snag about the ski-annexe. I'd never thought that the two companies might not mix on certain occasions.

'But now, what about the children's stockings? Perhaps we had better get their presents organised. It's getting late.'

Together they did what was necessary, and when they tiptoed from the children's room 15 minutes later, they left behind them three very bulging stockings and an interesting assortment of parcels—all sizes and colours.

After the supper trolley had been cleared, Hugh looked at Janice.

'I think you should get away to bed now,' he said. 'I'll wait up to lock the door, but there's no need for both of us to be late. Tomorrow will be pretty hectic, I should think.'

'It will be, but at least we're well prepared,' Janice agreed. 'Good night, Hugh.'

She set her alarm for half-past six, and when it roused her next morning she sprang up at once. Washing and dressing quickly, she hurried down to the kitchen to start the busy day there before the children were awake. By seven o'clock she had everything under control and she hurried up to the children's room, reaching it just behind Hugh, to find the children scrambling out of bed.

There was a happy hubbub as everyone wished everyone else a Merry Christmas, and in the general confusion Janice found herself being given a quick hug by Hugh. The presents were opened with shrieks of joy from the children, while Janice found herself presented with two attractive packages. They contained bath oil and perfume from the children and, most unexpectedly, a delicate little porcelain dish, hand-painted with tiny Alpine Gentian, from Hugh.

Janice stammered her thanks to him, quite overcome by such an exquisite gift. Beside it, her present to him of aftershave seemed rather feeble, but he seemed genuinely pleased with it.

Half an hour had flown past before Janice hurried downstairs again. The rest of the morning was spent in a jumble of turkeys, stuffings, brandy butter, mince pies and crackers. There was a festive air throughout the hotel and in spite of coping with a tremendous amount of work the staff found time for a good deal of light-hearted banter. Seemingly, the dance had been a great success. Iain was at the receiving end of some teasing from his friends as he had danced almost exclusively with the girl from New Zealand. When the dance had ended at half-past eleven, a whole crowd had piled into cars and driven to the Watch Night Service at Kirkton.

In spite of their late night, the boys were

full of energy and made short work of clearing up after the guests' Christmas Dinner.

In the evening, after the guests had enjoyed a cold meal, it was the staff's turn to eat. Hugh, who had spent much of the day with his children, taking them ski-ing in the afternoon, helped Janice to set up the tables. The children, permitted to stay up late on this special day, were dressing upstairs.

Soon all was ready. The cleaning women arrived with their husbands and the couple who ran the bar. Iain and his friends, Annie and Donald Mackay, Etta and her boyfriend, and the children, looking very smart in the clothes Janice had bought for them in Glasgow, all gathered, talking and laughing. Janice hurried upstairs, suddenly conscious of her unruly hair and shiny face. She'd hardly had a minute to herself all day, but instead of feeling tired she felt exhilarated and stimulated by the merry atmosphere. Feeling fresher, she ran downstairs again and there, at the bottom, talking to Hugh, was Sandy.

There was no time for dissimulation

and her pleasure in seeing him must have shown in her face, because he came to her at once, taking her hand in a warm clasp as he wished her a Happy Christmas.

Hugh's voice brought her back to earth.

'Well, time to get to work, Janice,' he said.

It wasn't till Sandy turned towards the dining-room that Janice realised he had been invited to join them, but when she brought in the soup, there he sat between Mary and Robbie, pulling a cracker across the table with Paul, and somehow looking just right in that family situation.

Janice's own meal was scrappy indeed, as she was seeing to the needs of the others, but there was a joy within her which had only a little to do with the general merriment in the room.

It was the change in Sandy's attitude which warmed her. However, it had happened, he was no longer cold or impersonal to her. His eyes were on her constantly, and when she met them with hers, there was no mistaking the warmth

236

of his glance.

The meal lasted for a long time. Most of those present had worked hard all day and were enjoying unwinding over this dinner. Janice lingered over her coffee, knowing that there was a great deal to be done before the day was over, but wishing to prolong this atmosphere in which she could talk freely and happily once more to Sandy. The children's presence helped to keep things on an unemotional level and they all laughed a lot.

Finally, the company began to break up and Hugh chased the children off to bed. Janice found herself quite naturally walking with Sandy to the door.

'Isobel phoned me,' Sandy suddenly said, after a pause. 'She explained that you're not planning to go back to London. I must have got hold of the wrong end of the stick.'

Janice stopped at the door.

'No, I've no plans,' she said simply, and he looked long at her, as if wondering how much to read into this.

Suddenly, he pulled her towards him. 'A girl like you,' he said softly, 'shouldn't stand in a place like that. It could be dangerous.'

His kiss wasn't long, but it was certainly effective. He was gone then, leaving Janice decidedly weak at the knees. It was not for a few moments that she realised what he had meant. There, above her head, dangled a bunch of mistletoe.

As Janice walked dreamily towards the kitchen and more work, the lounge door opened, and Mrs Rankin came out. Janice smiled at her, wishing her goodnight. She was sorry to see that there was no answering smile on Mrs Rankin's face. In fact, she looked distinctly displeased as she addressed Janice:

'The young folk are all away to the ski-annexe,' she said. 'A record session or some such nonsense. You'd think they could spend Christmas Night with their own folk.'

Before Janice could answer, Mr Rankin had broke in.

'Now, Nan,' he said reasonably. 'The young ones were with us all day. I'm sure no one else minded them joining some other young people this evening.' The phone rang and Janice hurried to answer it, thinking to herself that it was a pity Mrs Rankin couldn't relax and enjoy the event she had planned so carefully. The call was from Bryan. With a shock of guilt, Janice realised that she had not taken time to open the small Christmas package which he'd sent her. She confessed, pleading extreme business, but sensed that Bryan was, understandably, hurt by her neglect. 'Well,' she said to herself, as she hung up, 'he should have taken no for an answer!' But it was, for her, the one blot on a day of happiness.

On Boxing Day, Janice was off after lunch. She realised then how tired she was, and enjoyed lying down for an hour or two in the afternoon. When she rose, she had a long luxurious bath, using a liberal amount of the bath oil from the children. When she went down to tea, she felt completely restored, and was delighted when Isobel phoned briefly to ask if Mark and she could call in that evening.

After tea, Janice spent an hour or so with the children in their room, when they showed her all their presents. She supervised their baths, and saw them into bed at a fairly early hour, to make up for their late night the day before.

'Do you know any more stories about step-mothers?' Mary asked.

'About a nice kind one, maybe?' Robbie suggested.

Janice racked her brains, but couldn't think of one.

'I'll read to you from one of your Christmas books,' she suggested instead.

When she left them to sleep, she went to her room. It had been neglected lately, as she had been so busy, and she wanted to tidy it as she would entertain Mark and Isobel there later.

Returning along the passage, she reached the children's door, which was ajar, and she paused as she heard their voices, arguing. She was about to go in to quieten them when she heard her own name.

'But Daddy did cuddle Miss Janice. I saw him!' This was Robbie.

'Yes. And he used to cuddle Mummy. He doesn't usually cuddle women,' Mary added.

'But it was Christmas, so it doesn't really count,' Paul objected. 'People are always kissing and cuddling at Christmas. It's called the Christmas Spirit.'

'It would be nice to have Miss Janice for our step-mother all the same.' Robbie's voice was wistful.

Janice felt a sudden lump in her throat, and her voice came out more sharply than she intended.

'Stop talking now!' she called. 'Get to sleep.'

As she went downstairs, she was thinking how easy it would be to love these children as her own. The arrival of Mark and Isobel broke in on these thoughts, and Janice hurried to welcome her friends.

'Come on up to my room,' she invited them. 'There are guests in the lounge.'

'I'll have a word with Hugh first, if I may,' Mark said. 'I want to discuss entertainment over New Year. Perhaps we can come to an arrangement.'

Mark went through to the kitchen, while Janice and Isobel went upstairs.

'Well, did you have a good Christmas?' Janice asked.

'Very nice, thank you. Mother and I had several people in for dinner. Mark was working, of course, but I went up to the dance last night.'

They chatted on for a while and then Trudi's name was mentioned by Isobel.

'She's away now. She flew home to Switzerland to be with her fiancé at Christmas.'

Seeing Janice's surprised glance, Isobel gave an embarrassed laugh.

'I'm afraid I made a dreadful fuss about nothing. Mark explained when I eventually gave him the chance, that Herr Traub asked him to take Trudi around while she was here.'

'I'm glad things are right between you two again,' Janice said, warmly.

To her surprise, Isobel frowned a little.

'I don't know,' she said, slowly. 'You can never put the clock back. I said some things I really regret now. I don't see how Mark can forget them just like that.' She paused, biting her lip, before adding quickly, 'Things just aren't the same, somehow. I've spoiled it all.'

'Give it time, Isobel,' Janice said. 'I'm sure it will work out for you.'

With visible effort, Isobel smiled at Janice.

'Enough about that,' she said. 'I've some good news. Mother is to record a programme with Frank Dale. If she comes over well, there could be many more!'

Janice was expressing her pleasure at this news when there was a tap at the door and Mark and Hugh came in. Hugh had a coffee pot and cups, while Mark had a tray of eatables.

'Never let it be said that we are the idler sex!' Mark declaimed.

They had a happy time together. Mark and Hugh had arranged to provide joint entertainment at the hotels over New Year. There would be a dance at the Euroscot and a Ceilidh at Kirkton House, to which guests of either hotel would be free to go.

When their visitors left, Hugh and Janice carried the cups and the pot to the kitchen.

'We'll have to be thinking about the Ceilidh,' Hugh said. 'Donald Mackay will play the fiddle, and there's a fine accordion band in the Glen. I'll get on the phone tomorrow.'

'What about Mrs Dawson?' Janice suggested.

'I doubt if she'd come here. You know how bitter she is about this place.'

Janice told Hugh the news about the pilot programme Mrs Dawson was to do.

'I'll maybe ask Mark to approach her about the Ceilidh,' Hugh said. 'She'd certainly be a great asset.'

He paused for a moment, before continuing thoughtfully.

'I like the set-up at the Euroscot Hotel, Janice. If I did sell this place I really wouldn't mind if they bought it. They're good people to deal with.'

'You haven't come to a firm decision yet?' Janice asked, tentatively.

'Not really.'

He turned away from her a little, and his next words, spoken quietly, came as a surprise to Janice.

'You present the biggest problem, really.'

Janice stared at him, her eyes wide,

and he turned back to look at her.

'I really don't see,' he said slowly, 'how I can possibly part the children from you.'

This echo of what had been in her own mind earlier in the evening left Janice speechless, and he continued, looking away from her again, 'I can't see any answer to the problem. The longer I delay, the harder the decision, I suppose. Do you know, when I was with them yesterday, they spoke about you all the time; wishing you were there, too.'

He looked intently at her again.

'I suppose they've come to depend on you,' he said. 'I suppose we all have.'

There was an appeal in Hugh's expression and Janice was moved by this, and by the sincerity of his words to her. She searched for the right answer.

'It's not all one-sided, remember,' she said slowly. 'You've given me a real home and made me feel part of your family circle this Christmas. It could have been a very lonely time for me this year.'

She was horrified to hear that her voice was shaking a little, and with great effort managed to change her tone to one of flippancy.

'Apart from anything else, you've kept me run off my feet. It's as good a way as any to stop someone feeling lonely!'

They both laughed, and the moment of tension passed, but Janice found her thoughts constantly returning to Hugh's words. She felt even more convinced that the Murrays' days at Kirkton House Hotel were coming near an end and, as she lay in bed that night, she couldn't help wondering about her own future. When she had told Hugh that he had given her a real home, she had spoken her deepest feelings aloud. If Hugh was worried about separating her from the children, she too dreaded the thought of such a parting. As her thoughts went round in circles, she tossed and turned. Sleep was long in coming that night.

The following day, the Christmas house-party was breaking up, and everyone was returning to their far-flung homes. Mrs Rankin, who had seemed so discontented throughout the whole affair, had miraculously changed her tune when she spoke to Janice before leaving.

'I've to thank you for everything,' she said with feeling. 'Everyone has enjoyed the reunion thoroughly, and they're all full of praise for the hotel. I must admit I was a bit upset by the ski-club being here over Christmas, but when I think about it, it really turned out to be a blessing in disguise. After all, it helped the young folk to enjoy themselves just as much as the rest of us. My nephew and niece from New Zealand told me today they'd never had such an enjoyable Christmas in their lives!'

As Janice replied, she thought what a pity it was that Mrs Rankin hadn't realised all this earlier, instead of fretting during most of her stay at the hotel. Perhaps she was one of those people who couldn't really be happy without something to worry about.

Although the hotel was still quite busy with skiers taking advantage of the good conditions, Janice managed to escape to the ski-slopes on occasion, to re-charge her batteries in the keen mountain air.

One afternoon, as she unfastened her skis from the rack on her car roof, a familiar Land-Rover drew into the car-park beside her, and Sandy climbed out, dressed for the slopes. It was their first meeting since the mistletoe-kiss, and Janice, to her chagrin, felt her face heat. However, she managed to greet him perkily.

'I didn't know you could ski!'

Sandy regarded her with raised eyebrows for a moment.

'Didn't you? Well, I'll have you know that I grew up right here, and was ski-ing on these hills before all this was even thought about. I may not have much style, mind you. Never had a lesson from any of those Continental ski-instructors, but I can still come down the hill fast enough to leave you standing, I guarantee!'

After a few runs, Janice had to concede this. Unorthodox as his style was, he looked completely at home on skis, and knew the terrain in detail. They made several good runs, completely relaxed in each other's company, until regretfully, Janice saw that it was time for her to return to the hotel. It had been a marvellous afternoon in Sandy's company and she treasured the closeness of the afternoon.

As he saw her off, leaning out of the car window to talk to her, he spoke of the New Year Ceilidh at Kirkton House.

'I'll see you there,' he promised, and Janice's heart sang as she motored down the Glen.

The plans for the Ceilidh were going ahead. Various local performers had promised to be there, and Donald Mackay was to be 'fear an tighe,' or compere, and Mrs Dawson had agreed to sing. It would be the first time she had entered Kirkton House since it had ceased, in such tragic circumstances, to be her home, and Janice couldn't help feeling rather apprehensive about this. She was such an unpredictable person at the best of times, and she had shown herself in the past to have this strange obsession with Kirkton House.

The Hogmanay Dance had been held in the new hotel, and New Year was brought in quietly at Kirkton House with the few guests who had chosen not to attend the dance. Soon after seeing the New Year in, Janice slipped off to bed. Too many late nights didn't combine well with the busy day-times.

The hotel was crowded for the Ceilidh on the evening of New Year's Day and the various artists were enthusiastically applauded by the appreciative audience. There was a fine mixture of traditional and modern, Gaelic and English.

Mrs Dawson, in a striking black evening-top and long tartan skirt, made a great impact when she appeared. Before she sang, she stood silent for a minute, until she had everyone's attention.

'This,' she said with a dramatic sweep of her arm, 'was once my home, and my daughter's.'

She paused, and Janice held her breath, wondering what was to come. Across the room, she saw Isobel, staring wide-eyed and apprehensive at her mother, who continued calmly:

'All this was cruelly taken from us. Until it is restored to us, we are as the Macgregors in my song—landless!'

With great solemnity, she began her choice, 'The Macgregors' Gathering Song.' She had the presence and the voice to sing it outstandingly well, but Janice felt that she had chosen unwisely for such an occasion. There were a few stifled giggles from younger members of the audience, and some embarrassed restlessness generally. Mrs Dawson perhaps sensed this because, when she appeared again later in the programme, her mood had changed completely. She sang a lively, tuneful song, in her usual vivacious style, and she won long and enthusiastic applause from the audience.

Janice was busy pouring coffee when Sandy appeared beside her.

'Phew!' he said softly to her, but Janice had little time to make any comment as there was too much to do.

Isobel and Janice also were able to exchange a few words. Mark was working, and unable to be at the Ceilidh. Isobel was rather quiet, perhaps a little embarrassed by the events of the evening. However, the rest of the Ceilidh passed without anything else happening to spoil the merry atmosphere.

Most of the other guests were leaving, thanking Hugh as they went for such an enjoyable evening. As Janice made her way to the kitchen to complete the clearing up, hard on her heels came Sandy.

'Look, I know you're busy just now,' he said hurriedly, 'but I want to ask you—will you come out some evening? When you are free?'

'I can't honestly say,' Janice began, but, seeing from the closed look which came over Sandy's face that he thought she was trying to put him off, she added very hurriedly:

'I'd love to come out with you, but could I let you know when I've arranged things with Hugh?'

'I'll phone you,' he promised at once.

When Hugh told her next day that there was a call from her, Janice hurried to the phone, full of expectations. But it was Bryan, not Sandy, on the other end. Phone calls and letters from London had been less frequent than usual, much to Janice's relief. She was convinced that Bryan was not for her, and had tried several times to put him off spending his holiday in Kirkton the following week, but he was adamant. However, Janice had sensed lately that his certainty about their relationship was wavering too, so now, she made a final effort.

'Bryan,' she said gently. 'I really don't think there's any point in your coming up here. You know that my feelings have changed, don't you?'

There was a pause.

'I want to hear that from you, face to face,' Bryan answered firmly.

'I asked you to give us this last chance, and you agreed. Don't go back on it now, Janice.'

The call from Sandy came later that evening and they arranged to go out the following night. As it was a Saturday, there was the usual Supper Dance at the big hotel, and they decided to go there.

It was a wonderful evening, and Janice remembered the first time she'd gone out with Sandy, in Glasgow. She had only recently met him then, but she had felt that she had known him for years. So much had happened since then; so much misunderstanding, and such a slow growth back to a friendly relationship.

Only one small thing prevented Janice feeling perfectly happy. It was the nagging remembrance of Bryan's forthcoming visit. Janice felt that she should tell Sandy about it, and explain the circumstances. Sandy would be sure to hear of it, and Janice dreaded the thought that he might misunderstand. Equally, however, she was afraid of spoiling their new beginning, afraid that she wouldn't be able to find the right words, and that the warm affection in Sandy's eyes would change again to wariness.

She finally decided to say nothing to mar the enjoyment of the evening and, later, when she was alone once more, she was glad that she'd made this decision. Whatever happened the following week, she would have this perfect evening to remember for a long time.

Hugh's family was arriving from abroad that week. He told Janice that they hadn't been able to find a suitable home, but that his father had rented accommodation meanwhile in Devon.

'My sisters are coming up for a few days, soon,' he said.

The children were intrigued by these unknown aunts.

'I can't remember them at all,' Mary said, frowning. 'They're twins like us, aren't they?'

'Are they the kind of twins who look the same?' Paul asked. 'Perhaps we won't be able to tell them apart!'

'I wish they'd come in the holidays,' Robbie grumbled. 'We'll be back at school, and won't see them during the day.'

Janice, naturally, couldn't answer their questions, and Hugh was amusingly vague about his sisters. They were so much younger than he, and had been abroad for so long.

It was another visitor who was very much in Janice's mind these days. Bryan's visit grew closer, and Janice found she was dreading it, not only because of the complications between them, but because the visit itself might harm her relationship with Sandy—a relationship which was frighteningly important to her.

When Bryan at last arrived, he looked anything but menacing. He'd obviously decided to enjoy his holiday whatever its outcome. The New Year Sale at the Store had been very hectic and he was determined to cram as much fresh air, good food and healthy exercise as possible into his few days' freedom.

While Janice was busy, he took lessons from the ski-instructor at the chair-lift. Although he'd never skied before, he tackled the sport with a characteristic determination, and when Janice accompanied him to the slopes on his third day, she was surprised to see that he was already fairly competent.

It was on the third evening, when Janice was completely free, that they had their serious talk. As always, when in his company, Janice realised how much she liked Bryan. She also knew, however, that if she'd ever thought of him as a future husband, these days were long past.

He had asked her on his last visit if there was someone else for her, and she had been unable to give him a definite reply. Now, over the supper-table in a small hotel in Blairochry, he put the same question to her.

She took a moment before replying. She must convince him by her answer that there was no hope for him at all.

'Yes, there's someone else, Bryan,' she told him gently. 'I don't know if it will work out, or whether he feels the same about me, but while I feel as I do about him, I just can't think about anyone else.'

'But if it doesn't work out—' Bryan began quickly, but Janice interrupted.

'No, Bryan! Even if it doesn't work, I now know how much I can feel for someone. I've never felt like that about you—or anyone else. You wouldn't want a half-hearted wife, anyway!'

Bryan's face looked hurt, and vulnerable, but as Janice looked at him, she knew with sudden wisdom that the wound would heal. He wasn't the type to sit and mope. He had tried his hardest to get what he wanted, but having failed, he would set his sights on some other target. With a rush of affection, Janice put her hand on his.

'Cheer up!' she said. 'You know it's not so bad. You'll find someone to console you. I wouldn't be surprised that if at this very minute, there's someone in mind!'

This shot in the dark proved to be amazingly accurate. Bryan started a little guiltily.

'Well, as a matter of fact,' he said,

self-consciously, 'a new girl did start in the Store at Christmas. Oh, I hardly know her, and I was thinking things might still work out between us—' His voice trailed off, and, seeing Janice's expression, he joined her in rather a shaky laugh.

Well, thought Janice to herself, when she was alone in her room. To think of all the worry Bryan caused me! I needn't have let it bother me!

But in her heart of hearts, she was delighted that he'd reacted as he did. Janice did not like the role of a heart-breaker.

Bryan enjoyed the remaining days of his holiday, his spirits mostly high. Occasionally, he would murmur some word of regret to Janice, or look wist-fully at her, but she felt that this was more for her sake than an expression of his deepest feelings. He asked her to spend his last evening with him, and she felt it was the least she could do. She would have to work till after dinner, but they arranged to go for a late meal to the Chinese Restaurant in Blairochry. As Bryan was driving back to London the following day, Janice volunteered to take her car.

Just around five o'clock that afternoon, Sandy phoned.

'Hello there,' he said quickly. 'Could I pick you up tonight when you're finished? It doesn't matter how late it is.'

Janice felt her heart plummet.

'Oh, Sandy, I'm sorry,' she said. 'I can't make it tonight.'

'Not even late?' Sandy's voice was full of disappointment.

'I'm afraid not. I've promised to go out with a friend tonight.' This was not the time, she felt, to mention Bryan. 'Would tomorrow do?'

'No. There was someone I wanted you to meet. Well, it can't be helped. I'll phone again soon. Cheerio.'

This phone call didn't exactly put Janice in the frame of mind to enjoy her evening.

'It couldn't have been so important!' she tried to persuade herself. 'But who could it be? He said he wanted me to meet someone—'

Bryan, as always, was amusing company, and as she was enjoying the food too, Janice found herself cheering up, optimistically promising herself that Sandy, when everything was explained, would understand.

When she and Bryan emerged from the restaurant, it was a chill, foggy night. The car was parked a little distance away, and Janice gathered her collar close, shivering.

'What a night,' said Bryan. 'Let's run!'

He put an arm round her, together they ran, breathless and laughing, towards the car. They nearly collided with a group of people coming in the opposite direction. Under the dim street lamp, Janice caught a glimpse of an attractive auburn-haired woman, and Sandy.

She almost stopped in her tracks, but Bryan bore her on towards the car.

When she looked back, the figures had become hazy in the swirling mist, like people in a dream.

She tried to convince herself that she'd just imagined it was Sandy, and anyway he probably hadn't recognised her.

But, brief as her glimpse had been, she

had seen the shocked expression on Sandy's face as she ran past, encircled by Bryan's arm.

Next morning, she saw Bryan off. The mist had lifted, and he had, fortunately, a pleasant day to begin his long drive South.

' 'Bye, Janice.' He gave her a quick hug. 'Let me know how things work out with this other chap. Lucky man!'

As Janice answered, Hugh arrived back from taking the children to school, and came across to bid Bryan goodbye. Before getting into the car, Bryan looked from Hugh to Janice, as they stood together. A look of comprehension dawned in his eyes.

'Look after her!' he said, significantly, to Hugh, and Janice knew he had jumped to the wrong conclusion, putting both feet firmly in it. As he drove off, Janice was conscious of Hugh's puzzled glance at her and, pleading cold, she hurried back into the hotel ahead of him. To her relief, he made no reference to Bryan's parting remark.

Sandy had promised to phone, and Janice waited nervously for the call.

When it came a few days later, it did little to cheer her.

'Did I pass you with some people in Blairochry the other night?' Janice asked. 'We'd been at the Chinese Restaurant.'

'Yes. I was with my sister and brother-in-law, and my father. My sister was just passing through. They'd been up at the Black Isle, visiting her father-in-law, who's ill.'

'Was it your sister you wanted me to meet?'

'Yes.' Sandy's voice was flat. 'But it wasn't important.'

There was a pause and then Sandy added, his voice sounding strained, 'Did you enjoy yourself with your friend?'

Janice rushed eagerly into an explanation.

'Yes, thanks. He had arranged the visit weeks ago. You see—he thought things might work out for us, but I knew they couldn't.' Janice drew a deep breath, knowing that she wasn't putting things very well. 'Anyway, he sees it my way now, and there are no hard feelings.'

Sandy's voice, when he answered, had

262

a musing tone.

'No hard feelings.' He paused before continuing. 'No deep feelings either, I suppose. That's the way you like it, isn't it, Janice? Having a good time, with no-one getting too involved—or too hurt.'

Janice was shocked by the hard tone which had crept into Sandy's voice, and she answered sharply:

'Perhaps it is. And I can't see any harm in that attitude. Can you?'

'No, I agree absolutely.' Sandy's voice was bland once more.

'Would you like to come out with me on your next evening off? I promise not to bore you by getting too involved.'

When Janice finally rang off her thoughts were in a turmoil. Sandy had wanted her to meet his family that last evening, but instead of this he had seen her laughing in Bryan's arms. No wonder the image he was building in his mind was the wrong one. He saw her as a flighty pleasure-seeker, anxious only to remain fancy-free.

If only he knew, she thought, I'd give up my so-called freedom tomorrow to become involved—really involved—with him.
263

At least he still wanted to see her, however much he would be on his guard. This was her one consolation.

CHAPTER 11

During the next day, Janice's friend from student days, Jack Laing, arrived with his wife and party of school-children from the Glasgow school where he taught. They were delighted with the hotel and the well-equipped ski-annexe.

The hotel itself was very quiet in a post-New Year lull. Hugh said that he expected this and that things would pick up again towards the middle of the month. It was, therefore, quite convenient that Hugh's sisters should phone that same night to ask if they could arrive next day.

The children were full of anticipation as Janice walked with them and Jet after school.

'Will they be here soon?' Robbie asked for the umpteenth time, only to be given the same reply.

'They said they'd be here by dinner-time.'

'I hope we're not in bed before they come,' Paul said. 'If we are, can they come up and see us?'

'Oh yes, I should think so. As long as it's not too late.'

The girls weren't too late, and the children were just into bed when they arrived. The first thing they did after greeting Hugh and being introduced to Janice was to ask to see their nephews and niece. As Hugh took them upstairs, Janice thought that however much the children had expected, these aunts couldn't possibly be a disappointment. Their frank manners and attractive appearances, quite different from each other, would appeal to any child.

Soon Hugh appeared down, alone.

'They're all getting on like a house on fire.' He smiled. 'I've given them ten minutes before they settle down.' Then he added, his tone self-congratulatory:

'I was right, you see. They are nice girls!'

He sounded triumphant that his memory hadn't tricked him.

During the next two days, the guests at Kirkton House enjoyed life to the full.

266

Jack, Kate and party were delighted with the excellent snow conditions and with their food and accommodation.

The twin aunts, Susan and Fiona, who had skied only on water previously, headed for the slopes in the morning, but returned in time to collect the children from school and spend the rest of the day till bed-time with them. Janice was glad of this as the staff employed for Christmas had returned to their studies and, with the ski-annexe full, she was rather short-staffed. She had managed to engage another local woman but as she wasn't free to start till the following week Janice was kept very busy for a few days.

This was the situation when Sandy phoned one afternoon to arrange an outing. Janice, fearing that an excuse, however valid, might very well end his invitations altogether, suggested that he might like to come to Kirkton for supper that evening. He accepted at once. Janice mentioned this visit to Jack and Kate, suggesting that they might like to come to the Residents' Lounge that evening after their meal. She felt that a little company would ease things between herself and

Sandy, and was sure that Jack and Sandy would get on well together, as they'd been contemporaries in their student days in Glasgow.

There were no overnight bookings in the hotel, and the four had the lounge to themselves for an hour. Jack and Sandy did indeed find they had much in common, and had actually encountered each other in various rugby scrums. Janice and Kate talked a lot about Kate's baby. She was missing him dreadfully, and was not sure whether to be pleased or hurt as, each evening, she heard from his grandmother on the phone that he was as bright as a button, and not missing her at all.

'Heartless little monster!' she said, tenderly, as she returned from the phone. 'A typical male, of course!'

As she replied to Kate, Janice's ear caught something which the men were saying, and she turned towards them. Jack had been describing the part of Ayrshire where he grew up, and Sandy had been asking interested questions about the area.

Now, looking at Janice, Sandy

remarked:

'It's just possible I might be moving there. I have the chance of a job—Nothing definite yet. It sounds a nice part of the country.'

'It is,' Janice said quietly. 'A crowd of us used to go there at weekends, during our student days. Turnberry, Culzean, Dunure—it's all beautiful.'

Sandy gave her one of his long looks, and she gazed straight back at him. He seemed about to say something, but instead tore his glance away and spoke to Jack about something completely different.

Shortly after this, Jack and Kate took their leave, as they made a ten o'clock lights out rule over at the annexe. Sandy and Janice were not to have long alone together, however, as Susan and Fiona came in almost immediately, to be followed by Hugh, and then Isobel Dawson.

Isobel explained her reason for calling in so late.

'I've just been up at Mark's,' she said, 'and as I was passing the end of the road I thought I'd take a run up here. You see, we've only today heard that Mother's programme is to go out tomorrow evening—a week ahead of schedule. I thought you might be interested.'

'Of course we are!' Janice assured her. 'I'd have hated to miss it.'

The twins, of course, were interested to hear the story, and, when this was being discussed, Janice slipped away to bring fresh coffee. So Sandy was contemplating a move? It made little difference to her, she thought, as she felt that her own days at Kirkton were numbered. The twins had brought papers with them, and Hugh had been having long business discussions, with frequent telephone calls to his lawyer. Some decision, Janice felt, was imminent.

When she returned with the fresh coffee, Sandy rose to go. Janice could hardly abandon the coffee pot and follow him, so she had to let Hugh see him out.

The twins were talking about the children.

'We're thrilled with them,' Susan said to Isobel. 'They're such interesting children, always coming out with some idea.'

'Of course, you're their teacher,' Fiona said. 'They must keep you on your toes!'

'They do indeed.' Isobel smiled. 'but the best thing of all is the change in Mary.'

Briefly, she explained what difficulties Mary had experienced after her mother's death, and how she had overcome them.

'Janice must take most of the credit for that,' said Hugh, who had re-entered the room, smiling at her.

Janice protested, but Isobel and Hugh insisted.

'In fact, you've been a great blessing to all the children,' Hugh said sincerely.

Janice was amazed. Hugh was seldom so forthcoming, especially in company. She supposed that the rediscovery of his sisters had made him more open, more relaxed, within a family circle.

She felt herself colour a little as she made some reply. She did not miss, however, the significant glances which passed between Susan and Fiona. Surely they too were not jumping to conclusions!

When Isobel rose to go, Janice walked out with her to the car.

'Bring Mark some evening,' suggested Janice. 'You know how well he and Hugh get on.'

'Yes, I will,' Isobel promised, but her voice was listless.

'Are things back to normal again?' Janice asked, gently.

'To tell you the truth, I don't know. Mark seems so pre-occupied lately, and he never mentions the future. I'm beginning to think I'm just some sort of second-best for him. He can't have Trudi Traub, and I'm next in line! I just don't seem to get through to him these days.'

To Janice's distress, Isobel's voice broke as she hurriedly climbed into her car, and drove off.

CHAPTER 12

Janice's feeling that some decision about the future of Kirkton House Hotel would be reached very soon proved to be correct. The morning after Isobel's visit, things started moving very swiftly indeed.

When Janice had finished her breakfast, Hugh asked her to come to the office while Susan and Fiona took the children to school.

'It's time I let you know what's happening,' he said, 'although there's nothing definite yet.'

Janice looked at him in silence.

'You've decided to sell?'

Hugh nodded, not looking at her.

'I'm meeting Herr Traub this morning, and if a phone call from the South about ten o'clock gives me the news I expect, I'll offer to sell Kirkton House to the Euroscot Group.'

'Where shall you go?' she asked.

'That's what the phone call will tell me,' Hugh explained. 'You know that my parents and sisters have been looking for somewhere in the South of England? Well, a suitable place has cropped up, it's a few miles from the coast in Devon and will make an ideal guest house. There's a bit of ground, where my sisters hoped to start a small riding-school. The snag was that it's just a bit expensive for them and that's where I come in.'

He looked at her, as if appealing for her understanding.

'I know you may think it strange that I've changed my mind so completely over the past two months. I even remember telling you that no-one would make me give up my lifestyle here and that I was determined to make a go of the hotel!'

He smiled at her ruefully, and continued:

'It's only in the past few weeks that I've realised that this kind of life isn't really for me. I miss my painting more than I thought possible. And you've shown me that I must give more time to my children. Also,' he paused, frowning,

274

as if searching for words, 'I suppose, in a way, I've proved what I set out to prove —that the ski-annexe could be a success, just as Sheila planned it. It was her dream, and I felt I had to carry it through the way she wanted it.'

'What will happen to it now?'

'Well, Herr Traub is most interested in it, and he'll certainly incorporate it in his plans for the development of the area. Anyway,' Hugh's tone became confidential, 'I'm not giving up all say in the future of Kirkton House. The shooting and fishing rights here, which the Euroscot Group as so anxious to acquire, give me good bargaining power. In fact, I expect to raise the extra capital we need for this Devon property and still keep an interest in the development here.'

'And this place in Devon. Do you all plan to live together?'

'If we get it—and the phone call will tell me soon, although I think it's pretty definite now—that would appear to be ideal. There's the main building, where my parents will live, and which should make a most attractive small guest-house. There's a small stable block with a couple of rooms above, which Fiona and Susan have booked. Then, there's a cottage which will suit myself and the children. I shall work on the illustrations for my colleague's book, and give a hand where needed!'

All the time Hugh had been talking, Janice had been fighting her own feelings of desolation and emptiness.

'It will be good for the children,' she said.

Hugh looked at her for a moment. 'They'll miss you,' he said.

'What will you do?'

'I don't know, really,' she answered, making her tone as off-hand as she could manage.

'I'm sure Herr Traub would be delighted to give you a job—either here, or in one of the Group's other hotels in Europe.'

'Not here,' Janice said, suddenly. 'It would be better to get right away.'

'Janice—' he began, a note of concern in his voice.

The phone rang, and as Hugh turned to answer it, Janice quietly left the room.

In the kitchen, Etta looked with

concern at her pale face. 'Are you feeling all right, Miss?' she asked kindly.

'Yes, thanks, Etta.'

As Janice smiled at the girl, she wondered what the changes would mean to Annie and Etta. Would their jobs still be secure?

As she looked consideringly at Etta, thinking how her skill had developed lately under her own and Annie's tuition, she noticed that, as the girl prepared to do some baking, she was slipping a new shiny ring from her left had.

'Etta!' she said in surprise. 'I didn't know you'd got engaged! When did this happen?'

'Well, it was at the New Year really,' Etta replied shyly. 'But we didn't manage time to buy the ring till yesterday.'

When Janice had admired the ring and expressed her good wishes, she asked: 'Your fiance's a gamekeeper, isn't he?'

'Yes, he's under-keeper at the Rampton Estate,' Etta replied, her face clouding a little. 'But it's been bought over by the next estate, and Angus doesn't know whether he'll be kept on.'

Janice's heart sank. Little did Etta know that much the same situation existed with regard to her own job.

'Come to the office again, please,' Hugh called to Janice with a note of excitement in his voice.

As Janice followed him, she could tell from his attitude that the phone call had brought the news he had hoped for, and as they reached the office he confirmed this.

'We've got it!' he announced triumphantly. 'That was my father on the phone.'

Susan and Fiona were in Hugh's office, chattering excitedly. With an effort, Janice attempted to match their mood of celebration, and she must have achieved some success as they obviously noticed nothing strained in her manner. They planned to start for the South early next morning.

After a short while, Hugh shooed them from the office.

'I've a meeting with Herr Traub in a few minutes,' he explained, 'and he's always punctual. Janice, once we've dealt with the financial matters I'd like you to join our discussion. Herr Traub would certainly value your opinions—and there's your own future to discuss.'

'It's what we've dreamed of, isn't it, Susan?' Fiona said as they made their way from the office.

'Father and Mother are thrilled, too.' Susan added. 'I think Dad was a bit depressed to be retiring at his age. This will give him a real interest. He'll love playing Mine Host.'

'And Mum will be so happy to have the children near,' nodded Fiona. 'She's dying to meet them, and she certainly won't be disappointed with the way they're growing up.'

Then, at the same time, they seemed to remember that Janice wasn't included in the plans. Their expressions changed as they looked at her.

'You'll miss them terribly, won't you?' Fiona's voice was sympathetic.

'And they'll miss you,' Susan said. Then she added, with a mischievous note in her voice, 'Perhaps they won't have to be without you!'

Janice was aware that Fiona was darting a warning look at her sister, as she added hurriedly, 'Janice will come and see us when we've settled in. Won't you, Janice?'

Janice agreed and soon after this excused herself, saying that she had work to do. As she busied herself in the kitchen, she felt completely exhausted.

When she was called to the office again, Janice took with her some coffee and biscuits.

'Well, Miss Taylor,' Herr Traub said. 'What do you think of the news?'

'I think Hugh has probably made the right decision for the family,' Janice replied, cautiously.

'But what of yourself?'

'I'm sorry, of course. I've enjoyed my job here.'

Herr Traub nodded. 'And you have done it well. What do you plan to do now?'

'I don't know. Find another job, certainly.'

'Why don't you work for us! I can offer you a job here, or in almost any country in Europe! What do you say?'

'I'm grateful, Herr Traub, but I don't want to make any decisions at the moment. Can we leave it for a few days?'

Herr Traub looked at her, and seemed to sense her feelings.

'Certainly! Certainly!' he assured her. 'You mustn't decide such things without careful thought. Now, Hugh will tell you of our decisions.

Briefly, Hugh put Janice in the picture. He had sold out to the Euroscot Company, but had retained a share in the Scottish branch, which would give him a voice, though small, in policy decisions.

'The ski-annexe will continue,' he explained to Janice, 'and when the ski-ing season is over, Herr Traub plans to cater for parties of businessmen, providing them with a week of hill-walking, stalking and fishing.'

'What about Kirkton House itself?'

'Well, the kitchens will be used for cooking for the annexe, and the dining-room will stay,' Hugh explained.

'And the lounge, too,' Herr Traub said. 'As to the rest of the house, I have a plan. But no more can be said about this at the moment.'

He looked mysterious, and rather pleased with himself.

'What about the staff?' Janice asked. 'Will you be paying off many of them?'

'Not one!' Hugh's voice was triumphant. 'It's the policy of the Euroscot Group to employ local people wherever possible, and Herr Traub is confident that the surplus staff can be employed at the big hotel.'

'Yes,' Herr Traub added. 'We find that local people are much more reliable. Hotel staff can be such a floating population. No sooner is everything working smoothly when someone essential develops the scratchy feet.'

This was the first mistake Janice had ever heard Herr Traub make in his normally impeccable English, and she couldn't repress a smile. Herr Traub beamed back at her.

'Now, Miss Taylor,' he said. 'Can you advise me? Would your assistant cook here be able to cope with the cooking for the annexe—with help, of course? I would very much like if Annie Mackay would join our staff at the big hotel.'

'I'm sure Etta could manage,' Janice assured him. 'She's very capable and is a good cook now. She's engaged to be married, by the way, to a gamekeeper. She was telling me this morning that the estate where he works has been bought over, and his job's a bit uncertain at the moment.'

'So!' Herr Traub seemed very interested. 'A gamekeeper, eh? I was saying to Hugh that we must look out for such a one, to take charge of the fishing and shooting side of things. I must have a word with your Etta.'

'Shall I send her in?' Janice asked, rising. She was pleased that things seemed to be working out so well for the girl, whom she liked.

'One moment,' Hugh interrupted, diffidently. 'I think, Herr Traub, that it would be only fair to consult Annie Mackay first, to see if she's agreeable to the move to the other hotel.'

'You are right, Hugh. We'll go at once to her home. We shall return to the Euroscot Hotel, where our lawyers will meet us and do the necessary paperwork. Then we can see Etta and her fiancé.'

All the time he was talking, he was gathering papers into his briefcase and by the time he had finished speaking the case was secured and he was out of the door followed by a bemused-looking Hugh.

By the middle of the afternoon, everything was settled. Annie Mackay, who had come on duty at lunch-time, had been a little uncertain at first. She had been in charge of a kitchen for so long that she was rather wary of losing her status. However, Herr Traub had soon convinced her that her skill would be fully acknowledged.

'Now we shall advertise not only "Continental Cuisine," but also "Traditional Scottish Fare." And so have the best of both worlds,' he had assured her.

Etta meanwhile was in a state of euphoria that all her problems seemed to have been solved.

Janice, the only one whose future was completely unresolved, worked on through this endless-seeming day, listening to everyone's happy chatter and joining in their planning. By the time she had finished clearing up after the ski-party's evening meal, she felt quite deflated.

She went up to have a shower before

watching Mrs Dawson's television début and as she passed the children's room the excited chatter she heard reminded her that their aunts would have broken the news of the move South. She took a deep breath and went into the room smiling.

'Miss Janice, isn't it marvellous?' Mary cried. 'All living together. Won't it be fun!'

'And the horses. It's going to be great,' Paul breathed.

'Jet'll like it there, too,' Robbie prophesied.

If Janice felt some hurt that they had absolutely no regrets about parting with her, she managed to hide them. She rejoiced with the children and then kissed them all goodnight before leaving them to make their goodbyes to Susan and Fiona who planned to leave very early next morning.

A quick shower refreshed her, and she hurried to the lounge to watch Frank Dale's show. She was joined by Hugh and his sisters, and also by Jack and Kate, whose stay at the ski-annexe was rapidly drawing to a close.

'It's been really wonderful,' Kate said. 'I feel really fit after all the fresh air and good food. If it wasn't that I'm longing to see Stephen again, I'd really be sorry to leave.'

'I hope he still remembers us!' Jack grinned.

Kate gave an anguished cry.

'Don't say that!' she begged. 'He couldn't have forgotten us already. Could he?'

She looked so distraught that Jack hastened to reassure her that he had only been teasing.

They all sat down to watch the TV programme on which Mrs Dawson was to appear. She was the last guest, but she was certainly worth waiting for. She looked very lovely, and sang first a solo and then a duet with Frank Dale, the host of the show. She was enthusiastically applauded by the studio audience and those in the Kirkton House Hotel lounge agreed she had given a flawless performance.

'I must give the schoolhouse a ring before the line jams!' Janice said. 'Would it be all right to tell Isobel your news, Hugh?'

'Oh, yes. It'll have leaked out by now anyhow. Give Mrs Dawson my congratulations.'

Isobel sounded very happy on the other end, and after discussing the programme, Janice asked if she'd heard the news about Kirkton House.

'No,' said Isobel. 'What news?' Janice told Isobel about the arrangements.

She went straight up to bed then, only looking into the lounge to bid Fiona and Susan goodbye.

As she lay in bed, she chided herself for her sadness. She had so much to look forward to, so much more than most other people. She had the promise of an interesting job in almost any country in Europe, but deep in Janice's mind was the thought that no one really cared what happened to her.

CHAPTER 13

The next day was the last for Jack and his school party. They had been fortunate with weather until then, and it was a blustery day with low cloud.

Janice had woken with a headache which persisted during the morning. It was Saturday, and as she was free from lunch-time she decided to go ski-ing, despite the weather.

As she drove up the road, she met several buses heading for home much earlier than usual, and guessed that only the most enthusiastic skiers would be braving the elements this afternoon. On reaching the car-park, she spotted the bus which transported Jack's school party to and from the slopes during their stay.

Janice ran over to the bus, where she found Kate and a good number of the school party, drinking coffee.

'Hello, Janice,' Kate said. 'Isn't this foul? And on our last day too. Still, we've been very lucky. I suppose the whole week could have been like this.'

'Is Jack still braving it?' asked Janice.

'Yes. He's taken the more experienced ones up on the chair-lift. Sandy was telling him the other night about the longer route down. They were going to try it if conditions were suitable.'

Just then, Jack and the rest of the party came tumbling into the bus.

'Did you try the long route down?' Janice asked Jack.

'No. We were quite glad to get down the short way! I think they'll be stopping the chair-lift before long.'

One of the boys was complaining to his friends in a voice obviously meant to be overheard.

'It's not so bad. I've skied in worse. You'd think we were kids, the way they treat us!'

Jack chose to ignore this outburst. Janice remembered he'd said the previous evening that one of the boys was an experienced skier, but that he rather over-estimated his capabilities.

As she crossed to the lift, she wondered if she was wise, but her mind was quickly made up. A voice hailed her.

'You're not going up in this!'

It was Sandy's voice, and it's rather bossy tone annoyed her.

'Yes, I am. I'll have one run at least. That's what I came for.'

Sandy climbed out of the Land-Rover, frowning at her.

'I'll come with you then, to keep you out of trouble!'

On the journey up, Janice felt her hands and toes go numb, in spite of her protective clothing. Her face felt as if the muscles were paralysed and she could never smile again. Reaching the top, she bent to fasten her skis, an operation which took longer than usual as her fingers were so stiff. Sandy knelt beside her and quickly clipped her safety straps to her boots.

It was then another figure appeared from the chair-lift, and Janice wrenched her attention from Sandy, because, with surprise, she recognised the complaining boy from the school bus.

The boy was bent, fastening his skis, his sticks stuck in the snow by his side. Janice slipped her gloves back on and, grasping her ski-sticks, skied over to him.

'Does Mr Laing know you're here?' she asked the boy, who stopped what he was doing and looked at her silently.

'You had better ski down with us. They'll be worried about you,' Janice told him, as firmly as she could.

'I'm going down the back route,' he said coolly. 'You'd better stick to the easy way.'

With an insolent smile, he skied off, leaving Janice speechless.

'Where's he going?' Sandy had to shout to be heard against the wind, which was now coming in powerful gusts.

'The back way. He is an experienced skier, Sandy, but...'

She stopped. During a moment's lull in the stormy weather, she had heard a yell. As they both listened, they heard another.

'He's in trouble!' Sandy said tensely to Janice. 'I'll go after him.'

As they set off, the storm which had been threatening for so long unleashed itself.

The voice came again, nearer this time. It was a very subdued youth who confronted them with great relief.

'I'm not hurt, really,' he answered their anxious queries, his voice coming in gasps against the wind, 'but I'm in trouble. I fell on this icy patch and wrenched my ankle a bit. I hadn't taken time to fasten the safety strap to my boot, and my ski came off, I've lost it.'

Without a word, Sandy skied on downwards, leaving Janice with the boy.

She tried to show a confidence she was far from feeling. The way the weather was worsening, they would be lucky to reach the bottom even if fully equipped and uninjured. She wished Sandy would come back.

Several minutes later, he did. He loomed up through the blizzard, using the giant 'Herring-bone' strides necessary when walking up-hill on skis. Over his shoulder he carried the lost ski.

'Thanks a lot.' The boy looked younger and very much humbler. He put on the ski, fastening the strap this time, but winced as he stood up. Janice looked at Sandy, whose face was serious and thoughtful.

'We're not going down,' he suddenly announced. 'Too far, and the gully down there is terribly exposed—a real wind-tunnel, and we'd never make it in this. Come on, follow me. Can you manage?'

The youth nodded, gritting his teeth as he pushed himself forward behind Sandy. Janice came after him. Where were they going, she wondered. Suddenly Janice remembered the last afternoon she had skied with Sandy. Conditions had been perfect, and as they skied down the back route he'd shown her the mountain bothy where he'd camped as a boy. It must be near.

Her deduction was correct.

Inside, the floor was dry, and some logs were stacked near the fire-place. Sandy at once set to work to make a fire, while Janice turned her attention to the boy, Jim, who had flopped down, white to the lips.

'Sorry about all this,' Jim said, gloomily. 'I was an utter fool.'

'How did you leave the school party?' Janice asked.

'Well, I was telling some of the lads that it would be quite safe to ski down the back way. We were supposed to be doing it today with Mr Laing, but he changed his mind when he saw the weather. Wise man!' He paused, scowling at himself, for a moment. 'Anyway, I said I'd a good mind to do it on my own, and they all just laughed. So I pretended I was going for a bar of chocolate, and just jumped on to the lift with my skis. I had one ticket left, and I think the man thought I was with you two.'

By this time, a fine log fire was blazing on the hearth and Janice began to feel quite warm and cheerful. Sandy pronounced the ankle only strained, and propped it up to rest it.

'This would be very pleasant,' Janice said, 'if only there was something to eat. I'm starving!'

Sandy glanced at his watch.

'Only three o'clock,' he said. 'Too soon to eat. 'I've got these.' He proceeded to unzip the large pouch on the front of his cagoul and produced a big packet of salted nuts and several bars of chocolate.

'They'll send out someone to find us,' predicted Jim, with all the confidence of a young person who had been well looked after all his life.

'Not in this, they won't. They couldn't risk any other lives in such a blizzard. Anyway, the chances of finding anyone in this visibility would be very small.'

Jim began to look really worried.

'I know it's my fault! But I didn't mean to cause all this trouble. Couldn't we try to go down?'

'Look lad,' said Sandy quietly. 'I'm on the rescue team for this area. I grew up here, and probably know the place as well as anyone. But I wouldn't risk going down in this. It would be sheer madness.'

As Jim stared at Sandy, the defiant look faded from his face. The quiet authority in Sandy's voice and his obvious knowledge of the problem seemed to convince him.

Janice rose and looked out of the small window set high in the side of the building.

It seemed that a hungry, cold night could be ahead of them. She should, it occurred to her then, be feeling gloomy.

But as she looked at Sandy and he suddenly smiled back at her, she realised that what she felt was happiness.

As the hours passed, the storm outside the bothy continued, but the three inside were warm and secure in their stout refuge. The log fire, though smaller now as they conserved their fuel to last the night, still glowed and flickered, keeping at bay the darkness which pressed on the window.

It was an intimate atmosphere in which conversation was easy and silences were companionable. Somehow, the dancing shadows conjured up memories of days gone by and it was of the past that they spoke.

Jim, the cause of their predicament, seemed to forget his worry and self-reproach as he described family holidays on the West Coast. Sandy also spoke of boyhood adventures, while Janice, who found any information about Sandy of absorbing interest, did more listening than talking.

Sometimes, when a silence fell and they sat staring into the glowing fire, she wondered if Sandy knew about the selling of Kirkton House Hotel and whether he had made a decision about his own move to Ayrshire, but she didn't raise either subject.

Around six o'clock, Sandy shared out some nuts and one of the chocolate bars. These they all enjoyed very much, but soon after this Jim voiced the thought in all their minds.

'I'm dying for a cup of tea!'

Janice rose and, with little hope, felt around on a shelf at the end of the bothy. In the gloom, her fumbling fingers came upon some things which she took over to the firelight to identify.

'Four tea bags!' she gasped. 'And some sugar—as hard as rock, but still sugar!'

An old tin, which had obviously been used for brewing before, was found at the side of the fire, and with the help of some freshly fallen snow they were soon passing from hand to hand a scalding, sweet, sooty beverage which to them tasted like nectar.

Not long after this unconventional tea-party, Sandy suddenly interrupted the conversation, his eyes fixed on the window.

'Listen!' he said, intently.

Janice and Jim stared at him, wide-eyed, as they strained their ears, but try as they might, Janice could hear nothing but the crackle of the log on the fire.

'I don't hear anything,' Jim said at last. 'What was it, Sandy?'

Sandy rose, and crossed to the steamed-up window, rubbing it with his hand and staring out.

'It's what we don't hear now,' he explained. 'The wind's fallen and it's not snowing. I can even see some stars.'

Janice was puzzled at this interest in the weather, and in the firelight she saw that Jim's face was full of disappointment at Sandy's remark. She guessed that he had been hoping that rescue was near; that Sandy had heard voices approaching the bothy.

Several times in the next hour, Sandy rose to gaze out of the window, but he gave no explanation of his behaviour.

After one of his trips to the window, he swung round and asked Jim:

'How's the ankle now?'

Jim, startled, carefully moved his

foot around.

'It's not bad at all,' he replied.

'Will your ski-boot go on? I noticed it gives your ankle very good support.'

'I think so.' Jim was obviously puzzled. 'Want me to try?'

Sandy nodded, and knelt to help him ease on the boot and lace it securely.

'Try standing up,' Sandy suggested then.

Jim did so, putting his weight on the weak ankle to test it.

'Just a twinge,' he reported. 'But what's all this about?'

For answer, Sandy crossed to the door and opened it. Janice rose, and followed him to the threshold. She looked, and gasped in wonder. A full, bright moon beamed from the sparkling heavens.

The snow caught all the brightness from the winter sky, and added its own frosty brilliance.

'It's as light as day!' Jim breathed from behind her shoulder.

Sandy laughed. 'Not quite,' he said, 'but light enough to ski down if we all agree it's a good idea. I wouldn't suggest it if I didn't know the route so well, but you could follow my tracks. What do you think? Shall we go now, or would you rather wait till morning?'

'Go now!' Jim blurted out. 'My family will be frantic.'

Then he stopped, and looked at Janice.

'Sorry,' he said. 'You must decide. What do you think?'

'I think we should go,' she said simply. 'If Sandy thinks it's safe, then I trust his judgement.'

All agreed, they quickly prepared for their journey.

As she skied downwards in Sandy's tracks, Janice knew that this was something she would never forget.

Down they skied, the complete stillness relieved only by the whisper of ski on snow, until they reached the front slope of the mountain and the short descent to the bottom station of the ski-lift.

As if waking from a dream, Janice saw below the dazzle of lights and the sound, carrying upwards on the clear air, of many voices.

'What are all these people doing here

at this time?' she wondered, dazedly. At that moment, someone looked up, caught sight of the three descending the mountain, and a great shout rang out.

The sudden transition from the peace of the mountains to the excitement below left Janice confused. Willing hands unfastened her skis, took charge of the sticks and thrust hot soup at her. All the time came questions, explanations, relieved laughter. She looked around for Sandy, but he, too, was surrounded by a crowd of well-wishers, while Jim was the centre of a circle of his school mates.

'Miss Janice!' a joyful voice called, and Robbie came worming his way determinedly through the crowd, followed by the twins.

Janice barely had time to hand the cup of soup to a bystander before she was engulfed by the collective affection of the Murray children.

'They were just going up to look for you,' Paul told her. 'The rescue team were to go up the chair-lift and try to find you.'

'We thought you were lost for ever,' a rather tearful Mary added, hugging

Janice fiercely with relief that she was safe.

'Och, I knewed you be back in time for Devon!' Robbie said.

Then Hugh was by her side, gripping her arm tightly.

'Thank God you're safe,' he said, and Janice was surprised at the emotion in his voice.

'I wasn't in any danger,' she assured him.

'Come on home, I'll take you,' Hugh added, 'Jack can bring your car.'

Jack Laing and his wife Kate nodded agreement.

Doing as he bade her, Janice allowed herself to be led to the car. Hugh's arm still encircled her, while Robbie clung to her hand, the twins also pressing close.

'All right, Janice?'

Sandy's voice made Janice turn gladly towards him, but somehow Hugh's arm was in the way. She began to reply when, to her surprise, Hugh cut in, saying rather possessively:

'She'll be fine. We'll look after her now, thanks.'

With a brief goodnight, Sandy turned

away, and Janice found herself in the Land-Rover by Hugh's side.

'Hugh,' she said urgently, when she had collected her thoughts, 'do the children think I'm...?'

'Not now, Janice.' Hugh's answer was soft. 'Don't talk about it tonight. We'll straighten it all out tomorrow. It's too late now, and they've had about as much excitement as they can take.'

Janice realised the truth of this, but she had to know more.

'How can they think I'm coming with you?' she whispered back, as the children chatted happily to one another. 'Who told them?'

'No-one.' Hugh's voice was weary. 'I didn't realise what they were thinking until tonight. I suppose it's just that no-one said you weren't coming, and so they assumed you were. They think of you as part of the family, you know.'

Janice was silent. This explained the children's attitude the previous evening, when they discussed the news with her. They had taken it for granted that where they went, she would go too.

The rest of the evening was a blur.

Janice all at once realised how weary she was, and felt amazement on discovering that it was not yet ten o'clock. The children, quiet and tired now, went off to bed almost at once, and Janice was not far behind them.

For a while she lay puzzling over the best way to break the news of the coming parting to the children, but her final thought, before falling deeply asleep, was of Sandy. Somehow, she must put matters straight with him as soon as possible. She could not leave him thinking that her future was decided— that it lay in Devon with the Murray family.

CHAPTER 14

Next morning, while Hugh took his family to Sunday school, Jack and the school party prepared to leave. They had all enjoyed their stay very much indeed. Jim came to say a special goodbye to Janice. Before leaving, he pressed some money into her hand.

'That's for tea-bags and sugar,' he said. 'I'd like to replace them in the bothy myself, but I've got to go. Could you manage? Perhaps someone else will be as glad of them as we were last night!'

Jack and Kate were warm in their invitation to Janice.

'You'll come and stay soon, won't you?' Kate pressed.

Janice returned slowly to the hotel kitchen. Etta was busy there. She and her fiancé had done a great deal of planning since last she spoke with Janice.

'We're getting married very soon,' she

explained. 'Herr Traub's offered us accommodation here. I'm going to start living-in whenever the Murrays leave, and we'll get married at the end of February. I just can't believe things have worked out so well! Angus is fair pleased about getting the job here.'

Janice was glad that Etta's chatter required very little reply from her. Most of her mind was taken up with thoughts of the coming discussion with the children, for she was determined that they must be told the truth as soon as possible. However, she was not to have her way immediately. When Hugh and the children returned from church, Hugh had time only for a quick lunch before driving up to the big hotel.

'I've a business meeting with Herr Traub and Mark Proctor,' he told Janice hurriedly.

'What about the children?' Janice asked. 'Shall I try to sort out this mix-up about Devon this afternoon?'

'Leave it just now,' he answered. 'We should have a talk first. There's no hurry.'

Janice felt that there was every reason

to tell them as soon as possible.

The fine weather of the previous night had continued and Janice took the children and Jet for a walk up the hill behind the hotel. She tried to keep the conversation well away from the approaching move and for a while she succeeded.

The children were running ahead, throwing sticks for Jet to retrieve, and clambering over or jumping from rocks. High above the hotel, Janice looked down on the district which had become dear to her during the past months; Kirkton House, its pleasant lines blending so well with its surroundings, the cluster of the church, school and post office down the winding road beyond, and the snaking Glen road, carrying the eye to the sterner landscape of icy mountains.

What of Kirkton House now, Janice wondered.

Perhaps affected by her stillness, the children came and stood beside her. Mary slipped a hand into hers.

'We liked living here,' she said, rather wistfully.

'Did you like it here, Miss Janice?' Robbie asked.

'Yes. Very much.'

'Will Devon be just as nice?'

'Of course it will!' Paul broke in, impatiently. 'Better even. With the ponies, and Aunt Fiona and Aunt Susan.'

'I wonder what Grandma and Grandpa will be like,' Mary said. 'We've never seen them. But they always write us interesting letters.'

'And send super presents.' Paul, as usual, was practical in outlook.

'Will you be helping with the ponies, Miss Janice? Aunt Susan's going to teach us to ride.'

The question, thrown in casually by Mary, decided Janice. She would not deceive the children with half-truths. She chose her words carefully as she answered.

'I don't know very much about ponies. But I'll certainly have a ride when I come to see you in the summer. You'll all be quite good little riders by then, and you can teach me what to do.'

There was silence. Three pairs of eyes

stared at her.

'In the summer?' Robbie's voice squeaked with indignation. 'That's ages away. You're coming with us in a wee while—not in the summer!'

'Yes—we're all going, Aunt Susan said, and that means you, too,' Paul argued.

Mary was silent, looking at Janice with apprehension.

'What your aunt meant was that all your own family would be together,' Janice explained. 'You'll have Susan and Fiona, and your Grandma and Grandpa, and Daddy, of course.'

'And Jet,' Robbie added automatically, before bursting out: 'But we want you to come, too!'

'Yes,' Mary said, urgently. 'Please come too. I'm sure Daddy will say it's all right.'

'I'm sorry. I just can't.' Janice's voice was quiet, but quite final.

Suddenly, Robbie burst into noisy tears, to be joined by Mary, and then even by Paul. For a moment Janice was horrified by the violence of their reaction to her news, but even as she comforted them, passing round tissues to mop eyes and blow noses, she knew that, soon, all would be well.

After they had returned to the hotel, the children now dry-eyed if a little woebegone, Janice decided to phone Sandy. She must not let him go on believing she was going with the Murray family to Devon, and all that this move would imply. As she dialled the number, she rehearsed what she would say.

It was Sandy's partner who answered the phone and, to Janice's queries, he replied that Sandy had taken some days due to him and had gone off.

'I think he has some business in Ayrshire,' was all the information Janice could obtain regarding his probable whereabouts.

Janice replaced the receiver gently, and stood for a moment, gripped by disappointment. She had been determined that, for once, she would make a move towards Sandy. Now there seemed to be little hope of reaching him in the immediate future, and every day that passed would be another during which Sandy would believe that she was going with the Murray family to Devon.

Numbly, she went to prepare a meal. The ski-annexe was vacant that night, the next booking being for the following weekend. Nor was there any residents in the house during this lull which came after New Year. Hugh had stopped taking bookings for the Hotel now, although the ski-annexe would continue as usual.

She was busy in the kitchen, the children playing in their room, when Hugh arrived back from his meeting with Herr Traub.

'Is everything settled?' Janice asked him.

'Yes. It's most satisfactory.' Hugh was looking pleased. 'By the way, Mark and Isobel are looking in to see you tonight.'

'Lovely!' Janice said. She felt the need of some cheerful company. Then she remembered what she must tell Hugh.

'Hugh,' she said, and hesitated. 'I know you told me to say nothing to the children about Devon—about my not coming with you, I mean, but I had to. They began to speak about it while we were having our walk, and I couldn't deliberately deceive them. They were upset, but I think they'll soon get over it.'

Hugh was speechless for a few moments, and Janice at first thought he was annoyed that she had gone against his advice. Then she saw it was not annoyance which moved him, but something else.

'Janice,' he began. 'I'd hoped you wouldn't have to tell them you weren't coming with us.'

'What do you mean?' Janice asked.

Hugh's impatient tone took her by surprise, 'Look—we can't talk here. Come to the office for a minute. I've something to say to you.'

His strong arm propelled an amazed Janice into the office, where he swung her round, looking down at her searchingly.

'Come with us, Janice.' His voice had a softer tone now. 'Come with us to Devon. You know what I'm trying to say, don't you? I want you to marry me, Janice, and stay with us.'

Janice looked up at Hugh's face, so

close to her own. It would be easy, she thought, to say yes; to be welcomed with love into that family where, even now, she almost belonged.

She did love the children. She knew she could be a good mother to them, helping them along the path to independence and maturity.

She moved away from Hugh then, to cross slowly to the window. It was chill and dark outside, while inside the room was warmth and comfort. Should she settle for the cosy security of the Murray family or face alone the prospect of a future which might prove to be lonely and bleak?

Hugh spoke again, 'I know I've taken you by surprise. Don't give me an answer now. Think it over.'

Janice turned to look at him. She felt deep affection, even a kind of love, for him. She suspected that his feelings for her were similar. Theirs would be an easy, companionable marriage, with no great heights and no great depths. Hugh's passion had been spent on the wife he'd lost, just over a year before. In this second marriage, he would look for comfort, affection and, above all, a good mother for his children.

She could be what he wanted, she felt; but she had it in her to be so much more.

'Hugh,' she said, feeling very sad. 'I can't. I'm very fond of you, but I don't feel enough to marry you.'

He crossed to her eagerly. 'If you're fond of me, and love my children, isn't that enough? I'm sure I could make you happy. I didn't realise how fond of you I've grown till you went missing on the mountain. Please think it over. I'm sure we could make it work.'

Janice looked at him, searching for words to make him understand.

'Hugh,' she said, 'please understand. I must love someone the way you loved Sheila.'

He flinched and moved abruptly away. Janice waited silently until he spoke again.

'Yes,' he said huskily. 'I do see. I was lucky enough to find that kind of love. I hope you're as fortunate.'

At his answer, Janice felt tears rush to her eyes. She hadn't realised till then how afraid she was of losing his understanding and friendship. She smiled rather shakily at him.

'I had better see about that meal,' she said, and left him.

That evening, there were a few tears again at the children's bedtime, but Janice felt that already the children were adjusting to the situation. She was more apprehensive about their father. How would he act towards her now? Would he retreat into the impersonality with which he'd treated her when first they met?'

She needn't have worried. When she waited in the lounge that evening for Isobel and Mark to arrive, he joined her, and his manner towards her was, if anything, more friendly than before. He told her that, as nothing now kept him at Kirkton, he was anxious to move just as soon as possible. He meant to make travel arrangements the following morning.

'Will you be able to stay here over the transitional period?' he asked her. 'Etta will be living-in for company.'

'I can stay,' Janice assured him. 'I've not yet made up my mind where to look for work. I'm in no desperate hurry.'

They discussed various matters relating to the business until Isobel and Mark arrived.

One look at the new arrivals told Janice that they, at least, had no doubts about the future. Seldom had she seen a happier couple.

'Janice!' Isobel said, giving her an impulsive hug. 'How are you? None the worse of your adventure last night?'

When Janice had re-assured them and recounted once more the whole incident, she smiled at them both and remarked:

'You two are looking very pleased with life.'

They smiled at each other before Mark answered.

'Well, we are! You see, Isobel's promised to marry me.'

He looked at Isobel in such a way that a lump rose in Janice's throat.

'I'm glad. You're both very lucky,' she told them, thinking what nice people they were, and how well suited.

Hugh added his congratulations, and then Isobel broke out: 'But we haven't told you the rest of our news. We're going to live here, in Kirkton House!'

Janice stared at her, in surprise. Suddenly she had a mental picture of Mrs Dawson, standing there at the New Year ceilidh, proclaiming that the house would one day be restored to her family. People had been embarrassed, perhaps a little scornful.

'Your mother,' Janice said to Isobel. 'She'll be delighted!'

'Of course.' Mark laughed. 'She's got a bad case of the "I told you so's".'

'But how did this all come about?'

'Well, Herr Traub has asked Mark to take charge of this development. There's to be an Assistant Manager living-in at the big hotel. Herr Traub suggested that Mark might like to live here.'

'I jumped at the chance,' Mark told them. 'I'd been feeling a bit worried about my position lately. I knew change was in the air, but I didn't know how any changes would affect me.'

Janice remembered how upset Isobel had been recently, sensing Mark's preoccupation, and not understanding it.

'Anyway,' Mark went on. 'I wanted to ask Isobel to marry me, but I had nothing to offer her. The accommodation at the big hotel was fine for a single man, but not for a family.'

'The first floor here will make a lovely flat,' Janice said. 'I'm so happy for you! Things have worked out splendidly.'

'What does your mother plan to do, Isobel?' Hugh asked. 'Your present house goes with the school teacher's job, doesn't it?'

'I really don't know.' Isobel smiled. 'Mother is hard to keep up with these days. She's off to Canada soon, to tour the clan societies with a party. They've got bookings all over the country and may even go into the States! Anyway, she says her "Glen phase" is over.'

Although by no means grudging Isobel and Mark their obvious happiness, it did accentuate Janice's own loneliness in the days that followed. The parting from the Murray family came with startling suddenness.

Hugh phoning to enquire about taking his family and car by train overnight to London, where they would be met by Susan and Fiona, was told of a cancellation that very week. Apart from this booking, there was no other available for some weeks.

Preparations were hectic, but this was welcomed by Janice. The children had little time to anticipate the coming wrench, and when the evening of parting did arrive, they were too excited about the journey to be greatly upset.

Janice hugged them tightly, promising to visit in the summer.

'We'll take you out on the ponies,' Paul promised.

'You write to me—and I might write back,' Mary said realistically.

'I'll paint you a 'normous picture of Devon!' was Robbie's parting remark.

Hugh, giving her a brotherly hug, promised to keep in touch.

'I hope things work out for you,' he told her.

When Janice re-entered the hotel after waving them off, she felt utterly alone. Etta was out with her fiancé, and the house was deserted. Janice went into the lounge and switched on the television, staring at it unseeingly.

About an hour later, she heard a voice

shouting somewhere in the hotel. Alarmed, she jumped up to turn the television off, when someone knocked on the lounge door, opened it, and walked in.

'Sandy!' she gasped.

He crossed quickly to her. 'Did I frighten you?' he asked.

'A bit.' Janice's voice shook.

'Sorry. I had to come. Just arrived back from Ayrshire. I saw Hugh in Kirkton. He stopped to say goodbye and you—you weren't with him. He told me you were here, so I came right up.'

Sandy's hands held her shoulders as he went on, his voice unsteady.

'Janice, maybe you'll say I'm mad but I've been doing a lot of thinking. You keep shooting me down and yet sometimes, when you look at me, I think...'

His voice broke off.

'I'm probably making a complete fool of myself, but I have to tell you. I love you.'

The only reply Janice could manage was somewhere between a gasp and a cry, but he must have understood, for suddenly he was kissing her as if he'd been thinking of nothing else all the way

320

from Ayrshire.

After a while, he held her away from him and looked at her searchingly.

'I'm serious, you know,' he told her. 'I'm not one of your no-hard-feelings, casual friends. So think before you answer. Janice will you marry me?'

'Oh yes. I'll marry you,' Janice said.

There would be time for explanation, for going over the past and talking away the hurt they'd caused each other; time for planning the future and discussing the rival merits of Perthshire and Ayrshire; but that would come later.

For the present, it was enough that they loved each other, and were together.